M000074617

There's something magical about romance stories.

When we were little, fairy tales taught us that while there might be evil in the world, there was also good. To help us finish any great adventure, there were always friends. People who might not be exactly like us on the outside, but very much kindred spirits on the inside.

Romance adds the joyous promise that *everyone* deserves a happily-ever-after. I'm so glad you've got that magic in your world—the magic of romance.

As a special treat for Coastal Magic, I'm pleased to share with you the first book in a new paranormal trilogy. Set in the far north of Canada, three polar-bear-shifter brothers are about to meet their destiny—nudged by their matchmaking, meddlesome grandfather! I hope you enjoy this story, and if you want to know more, you can contact me via my website or social media.

Wishing you and your friends, old and new, a wonderful convention.

Viv

Vivian Arend
Coastal Magic 2020
www.vivianarend.com

PRAISE FOR VIVIAN AREND

"Vivian Arend does a wonderful job of building the atmosphere and the other characters in this story so that readers will be sucked into the world and looking forward to the rest of the books in the series."
~ *Library Journal*

"Steamy and sweet complete with a whole host of colourful side characters and enough sub-plots to get your teeth into. A fab read!"
~ *Scorching Book Reviews*

"There's a real chemistry between the characters, laced with humor and snappy dialogue and no shortage of steamy sex scenes to keep things lively. The result is an entertaining, spicy romance."
~ *Publishers Weekly*

Silver Mine is an outstanding story. The author creates a world that invites readers for the ride of their lives."
~ *Coffee Time Romance Reviews*

Arend offers constant action and thrills, and her characters are so captivating and nuanced that readers will have a hard time guessing who the villains really are.
~ *RT Book Reviews*

Granite Lake Wolves

Wolf Signs

Wolf Flight

Wolf Games

Wolf Tracks

Wolf Line

Wolf Nip

Takhini Wolves

Black Gold

Silver Mine

Diamond Dust

Moon Shine

Takhini Shifters

Copper King

Laird Wolf

A Lady's Heart

Wild Prince

Borealis Bears

The Bear's Chosen Mate

The Bear's Fated Mate

The Bear's Forever Mate

A full list of Vivian's print titles is available on her website

www.vivianarend.com

THE BEAR'S
CHOSEN MATE

VIVIAN AREND

This is a work of fiction. Names, characters, places, and incidents either are the product of the author's imagination or are used fictitiously, and any resemblance to any persons, living or dead, business establishments, events, or locales is entirely coincidental.

The Bear's Chosen Mate
Copyright © 2019 by Arend Publishing Inc.
ISBN: 9781999495770
Edited by Anne Scott
Cover Design © Damonza
Proofed by Angie Ramey, Linda Levy, & Manuela Velasco

All rights reserved. No part of this book may be used or reproduced in any manner whatsoever without written permission except in the case of brief quotations.

DATE: March 21
TO:
Cooper Borealis
Alex Borealis
James Borealis

*M*y *dearest grandsons,*
Before the year is done, I'll celebrate my
eighty-fifth birthday. I know you're all eager to find me the
perfect present. I have to say up until now, you're the best
presents I could ever have gotten. You've grown up smart
and strong, with real business savvy and enough cutthroat
ambition to make me proud. Borealis Gems is thriving
because of you.

You're also the most pigheaded and obstinate jackasses
I've ever had to deal with.

Telling me you want to focus on business and that
finding a mate can wait sounds impressive, but we all know
that's a load of crock. It's damn-well time you got your butts
in gear. I want to hold my great-grandbabies before I die, a
sentiment your grandmother fully endorses, as do your
parents—even though they're out of the country at the
moment.

Stubborn fools that you are, for years on end you've
resisted the mating fever when it's hit. Enough of that
nonsense.

There are nine months until my birthday. That's how
long you have to pick a mate, boys, or come New Year's Eve,

I'll arrange to sell my shares of Borealis Gems to Midnight Inc., and none of us want that, do we now?

When mating fever hits this time around, you decide. You can make an old man happy, (and your grandmother— don't forget Nana!) take full ownership of a multibillion- dollar corporation, and have the time of your life with a forever mate...or you can throw it all away. Your choice.

Don't make it a stupid one.

Regards,
Your long-suffering grandfather,

Giles Borealis, Sr.

∼

IN THE PRIVATE OFFICE ABOVE THE DIAMOND TAVERN, three decadent leather recliners were comfortably arranged around an oversized table. Perched on the edge of his usual seat, James Borealis let the handwritten letter flutter from his hand to the surface of the wood slab. He replaced the unexpected message instantly with a glass, tipping back the whiskey and drinking deeply as if he could wash away the bitter taste the proclamation had left in his mouth.

"It's *bullshit*." Their middle brother all but roared the words, his golden-brown skin flushed with anger. Alex dragged a hand over his military-style crew cut, leaving the dark strands upright. He snatched up his glass and imitated James, shooting back the contents rapidly.

They glanced at each other before slamming their glassware down a fraction of a second apart then twisting to check their oldest sibling's response.

Cooper had been the one to bring them together to

open the elegantly written missive from Grandpa Giles. Cooper was the one they'd always looked to for advice. With their parents traveling out of the country, he was acting CEO for Borealis Gems, his law degree and dedication to excessive preparation helping advance the company in myriad ways in the short time he'd been in charge.

Now his expression was cool and collected—far more so than James could manage, and usually *he* was the calm and collected face of the family company. Publicity and promotions were his delight, and he'd been damn proud to be able to step in and take over what had been his mother's domain for many years. Charming he could do. Eloquent— that was him. Usually.

Except right now.

The unreasonable demand rattled through his brain again, leaving him mentally staggering. A deadline to be mated? Who *did* that?

"Do you think he's serious?" Alex demanded.

"He's never had a problem with us being single before," James said immediately. "And what the hell was that nonsense about 'for years on end' and 'avoiding the mating fever'? Maybe it's true for you two, but I'm only twenty-six. Mating fever's only hit once before, and no way was I ready to settle down last year. Or this year, for that matter," he complained. "I hid out for the week like any sane male."

"The same way Cooper and I have for the past 'years on end,'" Alex noted. "Gramps isn't wrong about us not wanting fate to be in control of our destinies."

Cooper raised the glass in his hand, swirling the liquid as he stared into the amber depths. His dark hair was shot with distinctive silvery-blond strands that reflected the late winter sunshine pouring into the room above the Diamond

3

Tavern, the pub that James managed as a side business to the family mines. "Grandfather is getting older. Who knows what brought on the change? Truth is, he's issued an ultimatum. Now we have to decide what we're going to do about it."

Cooper's utter composure in the face of the unreasonable demand eased James's panic enough he could speak calmly. "Grandpa wouldn't sell the family business to our competitors."

Big brother raised a brow.

Yeah, he was right. The cranky bastard would totally do it just to piss them all off. "It's a good thing I like the old man, or I'd be tempted to rip his head off his shoulders," James grumbled.

"We got the stubborn part of our nature from him," Cooper said drolly.

Alex paused, adjusting position briefly as he reached into a back pocket to pull out his ever-present set of handcuffs and toss them on the table. Then he stretched his legs out, leaning back on the fine leather upholstery like a king on his throne, his arms spread wide on the high armrests. Even reclined he looked every inch the predator he was. Head of security for the family, Alex was lethal and deadly. Not just brawn, though. His mind was smart as a whip and misjudged at a person's peril. "What's the game plan, then? Because I will not let our company end up in the Lazuli family's clutches."

Intense, much? His middle brother's proclamation was over the top, but James had worries of his own. Twenty-six was way too young to settle down.

Mating fever struck all polar bear shifters in their prime once a year. In happily mated couples, it became a glorious sexual romp for a week.

For unmated males, the wild impulse still drove them to enthusiastic sexual exploits. It was nature's way of encouraging permanent bonds to form—because while people fell in love throughout the year, *mates* only happened during the fever.

Bonus—*or not*—the fever didn't just affect the male, but had an impact on the females around them, boosting their natural response. Mating fever wouldn't make a woman say yes when she wanted to say no, but it would escalate an existing attraction tenfold. Like bonus pleasure to make the situation more fun for everyone.

A week of down and dirty? Not usually a problem. But no male who *wanted* to stay single willingly hung around the ladies when the fever hit. It was too risky.

If there was a good match—by whatever standards the *woo-woo* of polar bear fated-mate-dom decreed—that week of sex was the beginning of the end. Like a shotgun marriage, they'd be stuck with each other forever.

Nope. The only impact James could see mating having on his life was a huge imposition on his time.

He didn't want a mate. Didn't need someone slowing him down and keeping track of him. Not to mention the likelihood of breeding. *Double shudder*. If there was some way to get out of it and still meet Grandpa Giles's demand, he was all for it.

Although, if I have to be stuck with just one woman...

He shoved the thought away, the way he had a million times before over the years. He refused to think of Kaylee in that way, no matter how much his inner bear insisted on turning pervy thoughts on high.

"It's simple, really," Alex announced. "We make James do it."

Getting indignant helped him avoid the truth still

buzzing in his brain. "Get the hell out. I don't want to settle down yet, and I'm the youngest. If anyone, it should be Cooper biting the bullet and carrying on the Borealis line."

Alex grinned harder. That option left him off the hook. "He's got a point—"

"I say we see what happens and let nature decide," Cooper interrupted. He drank deeply, finishing his whiskey and replacing the glass on the table with a soft *clink*. "We have no way of knowing when mating fever will hit next, or who. I suggest we all agree this time we simply let it run its course. One thing Grandfather didn't take into consideration: the mating fever isn't a guarantee. It's supposed to increase the chances of partners matching up, but if we're not with our forever loves, nothing will happen beyond a week of fun."

James stared at Cooper as the truth settled in hard. "You're...right."

His big brother snorted. "Don't sound so shocked."

Alex leaned forward, elbows on his knees as his eyes sparked. Considering. "So. This means the instant we feel the fever coming on, we need to get alone with someone attractive but most definitely not our mate."

"Now you're making this more complicated than it needs to be," Cooper pointed out.

Alex lifted his shoulders. "Just planning ahead, brother."

Cooper went on. "We'll see if any of us ends up with a mate by New Year's. Grandfather can't be displeased if we're *trying* to follow the rules. His ultimatum only says we're not supposed to fight the fever."

It was so like Cooper to focus on the legal loopholes.

He continued, "Who knows? Maybe one of us will end up mated, and the other two will decide settling down isn't the worst thing ever, and they'll vow to actively search over the coming year for their one and only."

It all sounded so reasonable...

Except James knew his oldest brother. "That last bit was bullshit, wasn't it?"

"Damn near one hundred percent," Cooper responded, a twinkle in his eye flashing as he winked. "I had an idea something like this was in the works, so I've given it a lot of thought. Grandfather Giles has got us where he wants us. He's no dummy. I can't see any way to keep the business in the family other than to follow his instructions."

Alex sighed as he leaned back and stared up at the ceiling. "So we let fate decide."

"Fate and the mating fever, yes."

It sucked, but Cooper was right. James slid to the front of his chair and held his hand above the table, the way they always had when making pacts as young cubs.

"No resisting the fever"—he repeated—"and we let fate decide."

Alex placed his hand palm down over James's. "We let fate decide."

Cooper eased forward, his bulk making the leather squeak in protest as he placed his hand over both of theirs and nodded once. "May she have mercy on us."

1

June 21, Yellowknife, Northwest Territories

*D*amn bear.

Kaylee Banks stared out the second-story window as the most beautiful man on the face of the planet, at least in her humble opinion, strolled toward the massive building that housed Borealis Gems.

He'd parked his private plane on the company airstrip, and she bit down on her lower lip to keep from moaning as, muscles flexing, the object of far too many dirty daydreams stripped away his jacket and loosened his tie, a patch of dark hair appearing on his chest when he undid the top buttons of his shirt.

The traces of civilization being cast off as James Borealis returned to the north.

She slipped out of the office space onto the balcony as she pulled out her phone.

Kaylee: _You're back early_

It was fun to watch the message arrive in real time. He fished his phone out his pocket. The smile that crossed his face was real, wiping away what had been a far-from-typical James expression as his fingers moved over the screen.

James: *Kaylee Kat. Where are you? Or are you a fortune teller now?*

Kaylee: *Look up.*

She waited until his glance rose far enough then waved.

He waved back. *What're you doing here at the office? Come to visit Amber?*

Kaylee: *Your grandpa hired me to take publicity shots over the next week so Borealis Gems can update its brochures.*

James glanced at his watch. He tapped a few buttons and checked the screen before shaking his head: *If you need outdoor shots today, you'd better work fast. There's a big thunderstorm rolling in this afternoon.*

Great. She let out a long breath. James was one of the few people who knew how uncomfortable she was during storms. They'd been friends for long enough; he knew a lot of her secrets.

A lot of her secrets, but definitely not all.

Kaylee: *Trust me, I'll make sure I'm hidden away somewhere safely before all the crashing and banging begins.*

He resumed walking, chin dipping in agreement even as he ran a hand over the back of his neck and down his chest.

His big hand distracted her in the wickedest of ways.

He'd rolled up his shirtsleeves, and his thick forearms were right there, mesmerizing.

She couldn't take her eyes off him, and maybe because she was watching so intently, it registered that something was wrong. He rolled his shoulders and stretched his neck, while that very unenthusiastic and untypical frown had returned to his face.

Kaylee: *You okay?*

James: *It's nothing*

Kaylee: *My BS sensor is pinging...*

James: *Fine. Don't know why, but I'm beat. A standard publicity run shouldn't knock me out like this. Kind of sore all over.*

Oh, the places her brain went. And the speed it went there—shocking, really.

I could rub out the kinks, Kaylee thought with a sigh. *Please and thank you. I could rub your shoulders, your back, or anything you need rubbed.*

Instead she went with something more logical than creepily offering to be his personal, private masseuse.

Kaylee: *Maybe you caught that summer bug that's going around. Why don't you go home?*

Kaylee: *Hop in the tub before the storm hits. That'll help work out some of the kinks left after being trapped in the Cessna for hours.*

For a moment, James seemed torn before he nodded firmly, staring up. He now stood directly below her, feet away from the side entrance. Close enough they could talk without raising their voices too much.

"You're right. I don't think there's anything dire I need to take care of in the office." His deep voice carried up to the balcony, brushing across her skin like a caress.

His hands moved quickly to undo the rest of his buttons, and a moment later he was draping his suit jacket, shirt, and tie over the handrail to the side of the entrance.

Her breath got stuck in her chest, and then, oh my God, it was a good thing she wasn't breathing because she would have moaned loud enough for him to hear. Right there, with her in front-row seating, he'd undone his belt, button and zipper, getting ready to drop his trousers.

Something of her stupor must've carried on the air because as he toed off his shoes, James paused. He met her gaze again, offering a boyish grin. "You don't mind grabbing my stuff, do you? I'd go tuck it in the clothing stash, but that's all the way back at the far edge of the airfield."

He stood there only partially clothed with the typical casual shifter attitude toward nudity, and she was one step away from fainting like some Victorian heroine.

It wasn't the getting-naked bit making her flush. As shifters, there was nothing innately sexual about stripping off clothes to make a shift to their animal sides. It was ordinary and simple. Natural and normal.

But *James getting naked* equaled *oh my God*. Her reaction to *him* was not normal by any stretch of the imagination. Thus, the blush, the shortness of breath, and the other physical reactions she was having in spades.

Her inner bobcat rolled her eyes.

The feline that was Kaylee's other self wasn't very

vocal. The cat tended to stay silent, but that didn't mean she didn't have *opinions*.

Other shifters seemed far more in touch with their animal sides. Kaylee wasn't sure if it was because she was a cat and most of her shifter knowledge came from bears and wolves, but unless she was in feline form, her cat remained mostly aloof and let Kaylee run the show.

It was good in some ways—no flying off the handle and having a hissing fit when something went wrong. But bad because there were times it would be nice to utilize her cat's assets.

The feline wasn't shy, not by any stretch of the imagination.

Please. Why should I be shy? The world exists for cats' pleasure. Everyone knows this.

Kaylee snickered, briefly distracted. *I wish you'd loan me some of your kitty mojo.*

Her cat sniffed daintily then went silent, obviously bored with the conversation.

No help there. Shifters might be two in one simultaneously—human and animal—but many of them found one half better at certain things.

Watching James Borealis get naked was not a thing human Kaylee did well.

Worse, there was no hiding the fact she reacted. The Borealis brothers had caught her blushing up a storm years ago and Alex had assumed her bashfulness was fair game to tease about. It was kind of sweet, in a twisted way, because Kaylee didn't have any siblings and getting teased was a form of family connection she'd craved.

Cooper had teased the least, turning his back when they shifted in larger groups, but James had jumped right in and followed Alex's lead.

Lately James's teasing seemed to hold erotic overtones—but that had to be Kaylee's feverish imagination playing tricks.

Wishing that he really was interested in her was wrong, considering she knew the two of them were an impossibility. Nope. He teased like any friend would, but they were never going to be anything more than that for so many reasons.

Which is why, while she didn't wish ill-health on him, she really hoped he was feeling out of it with his head cold or was far enough away to not notice how hard her heart was pounding.

"Earth to Kaylee. Did you hear me? Can you grab my stuff?"

Oops. Good grief, how long had she stood there daydreaming? "No problem."

She'd answered as if she wasn't panting from admiring all the nakedness appearing before her.

"Thanks, Kaylee Kat."

Watch? Or look away?

It wasn't really a question. Kaylee stepped a foot to the right to get a better view. She could blush while enjoying the show.

He went on speaking as he stripped. "Can you tell Amber I'm back but that I've gone home for the day?"

"No problem."

She knew those words were functioning. She wasn't going to try anything fancier.

Far too quickly, James was down to skin. Glorious bronze skin, tanned and touchable. Big biceps flexed as he moved, his beautiful pectorals shifting as well as her gaze dropped to the trail of dark hair that led down the center of his belly to his groin where the thick length of his cock stood erect and—

Oh my God.

Kaylee tore her gaze away, because nudity might be okay, but staring at the man's junk was not kosher.

Also, she was getting a little lightheaded.

He grabbed his pants off the ground and tossed them over the rest of his things with little care for the expensive fabric. Then he glanced up one last time and flashed her—

Oh boy, did he ever.

Bad brain. Bad, bad Kaylee brain!

—flashed her a sheepish grin. "Give me a shout later. Once I kick this bug, we'll have that movie marathon we talked about."

His naked butt flexed as he turned away from her gaze —*Lordy, his ass is a thing of beauty*—and strode toward the edge of the manicured lawn where it bumped up against the wilderness outside the factory.

A second later it was like trying to watch an optical illusion. A hue of multicoloured lights shimmered then a massive polar bear stretched lazily before ambling off into the trees.

Kaylee would never get enough of seeing him shift. Up close was even better. She sighed again.

"No problem," she whispered, although that was far from the truth.

There was a problem. A great big enormous one, one hundred percent on her side of the equation.

She was hopelessly, helplessly in lust with one of her best friends. He not only had no idea, but she was the last person on earth he needed in his life as anything other than a friend.

No problem? In her dreams.

2

_____

Cranky. Itchy. Pissed off at the world.

All of those sensations were running on high as James left the proximity of Borealis Gems.

He should be happy as a pig in mud right now. He'd had a successful trip to New York, sat through a half dozen interviews and talk shows, and successfully created more positive publicity for the family company.

Now he was home and back in the wilderness. The warmth of spring air wrapped around him, and scents filled his nostrils with green, growing things and the promise of a lazy day. This was paradise and should have cured whatever ailed him.

The itching ache at the back of his neck had increased, though, so he let his bear side take control, ambling in the direction his animal wanted to go. The human side of him had enough on his plate to deal with.

He shrugged his big shoulders, trying to escape the tingling sensation. It was strange—he didn't think the meetings he'd attended were that stressful. In fact, he usually gloried in getting to be in the public eye, which is why he did it rather than Alex or Cooper.

Maybe he *was* coming down with some kind of shifter flu, which would really suck considering their type rarely got ill.

Constitution of...well, a polar bear and all that.

But the back of his throat itched, and even though he expected his scent ability to be off the charts, one smell out there was just not right. The sweet, sharp fragrance had bothered him the entire flight home. He'd wasted time post-flight trying to track it down.

He'd wondered at first if one of their top-tier clients, the ones he'd just flown back to their home outside New York, had left something on the plane. But after searching under all the seats, he'd come up blank.

Still, that scent would not go away—and not only did it make everything about him hot, he found himself getting aroused at the most inopportune times. Thank goodness Kaylee had been thirty feet above him as they talked. It had made it easier for both of them to ignore his damn hard-on.

Wasn't the first time he'd had one around her by any means, but usually he could explain it away with a joke and write it off as a guy thing.

This one? Instant and outrageous, and while he'd liked to have blamed it on her, he wasn't usually *that* hair-triggered. They'd been standing outside his workplace, for fuck's sake, talking about innocent subjects, and he'd been so turned on that if she'd been within arm's reach he would've been tempted to grab her and follow through on the lust-filled thoughts he'd been fighting for years.

The thoughts he'd reconsidered and refocused on in recent months.

Slow. Take it slow, he reminded himself.

You no like slow, his bear grumbled. *You like Kaylee.*

Shut up, he told his bear.

Nope, wandering through the bush was the only way to get rid of this kind of frustration.

When James found his feet had unwittingly taken him back to the parking lot of Borealis Gems, he sat down at the edge of the asphalt and glared angrily at the vehicle in front of him.

Stupid bear brain. There was absolutely no reason to be sitting here next to Kaylee's dump of a truck. The one that made James angry because every time he side-eyed it, she insisted the vehicle could go another hundred kilometers or more.

Too stubborn to give it up, he assumed. The damn thing represented the first time she'd purchased something major without her parents' approval as a sixteen-year-old.

He got it, he really did. Her parents weren't the greatest, and everyone needed a *fuck-you* memento or two in their lives. But one of these days the POS was going to break down and he wouldn't be there to haul her ass out of trouble.

He snarled at the vehicle, got himself up and headed home to his recently finished apartment complex that overlooked the massive lake Yellowknife was built along.

It took deliberate thought to keep his bear self from looping back, so it wasn't until he was in his penthouse suite on the tenth floor, the door locked behind him, that he finally took a deep breath.

The tension at the back of his neck was huge and painful—this *had* to be some kind of polar bear flu.

He paced to the answering machine, the red blinking light taunting him. He had a cell phone, but as a shifter, it wasn't always on him, and people had to have a way to get a hold of him. He was stuck supplementing with old-school technology.

He clicked the playback button, rubbing a hand against his chest and over his arms in the hopes the ache would fade.

It was a message from his grandpa, time stamped from only a few minutes earlier. Must have come in while he was bear-ing it home.

"James, my boy. You've been busy the last couple of days. Good job. I just heard from our potential new investors. They were very impressed with your sales pitch." Giles Borealis chuckled, somewhere between conspiracy and amusement. "I almost feel as if I should've warned them ahead of time how convincing you are. It's good to know you've got what it takes to keep this company moving into the future. Well done."

Of course, well done, James thought. *Every time I go into a meeting, I pretend I'm you. No one stands a chance.*

He was planning on getting *What Would Grandpa Do* bracelets for himself and his brothers, and giving an extra one to the old man for a Christmas present. Grandpa would get a kick out it.

The message continued to play.

"Now, I don't intend to tell you how to do your job, but I did want to remind you, as good as you are at wining and dining our new investors and clients, you need to have someone shiny next to you at the Canada Day Gala. This is important, James. We've got potential sales that need to be finalized during the party. But of course, you know all this already. Just indulge an old man as he meddles. Not many special things going on in my life anymore. Not as if I've got grandbabies to enjoy, and there's a decided lack of female company at our family table. Your grandmother is feeling very overwhelmed. Do get on with finding a mate, my boy."

"Can't leave well enough alone," James muttered at the machine as his gave a quick, but cordial farewell, and the message came to an end.

Get on with finding a mate. As if the old man sending that letter earlier in the year hadn't changed everything. The ultimatum had been hanging over his and his brothers' heads since March.

James headed straight for the shower in the hopes that some screaming hot water might wash away the bugs currently rampaging through his system.

His secondary goal was to cool down his temper because while he loved Grandpa Giles, the old man knew exactly which buttons to push.

It was true—James *did* need a date for the gala event. He also knew exactly who he wanted beside him.

Again, partly Grandpa Giles's fault.

When James had first read the blackmail letter, he'd panicked. It was only after a week or so of mentally bitching about the pact he'd made with Alex and Cooper that he'd realized it wasn't the end of the world.

He'd been friends with Kaylee since second grade. He'd had rising sexual interest in her since they were teens, but their friendship had been too valuable to mess with becoming temporary boyfriend/girlfriend.

But if he had to spend his life with one woman? He'd pick her, every time. Smart, beautiful, willing to call him on his bullshit. She was everything he needed. Also, they were already good, good friends—which meant once they mated, they'd get to keep being friends forever.

She was perfect.

Grudgingly, he had to admit Grandpa's letter had helped him realize that.

Only, ever since deciding he was going to take charge of fate and *pick* his mate, he'd been shut down every damn time. Over the past three months he'd been making advances, in a casual "why don't we take this to the next stage?" kind of way.

He'd tried flirting. She'd laughed and rolled her eyes.

He'd tried stroking her arm casually while they watched a movie. Kaylee had picked up a cushion and started a pillow fight.

It seemed no matter what he attempted to move their relationship to a new stage—without getting creepy about it —she still refused to see him as anything other than a buddy.

He wasn't about to give up, but damn...this lack of forward momentum was hard on a guy's ego.

James sighed heavily. Truth was if she truly didn't want him as more than a friend, he wasn't going to bash her over the head and force her.

Bashing gently is okay, his bear offered.

No. No bashing at all, he snapped back.

Stupid bear.

It wasn't until the hot water was streaming over him and he was lathering up that he realized his cock was upright again, as if waving to get his attention.

Only sick fucker would get flu that makes massive hard-ons, his bear told him dryly. Snarkier than usual—probably pissed at being told no bashing.

Shut up, he told his bear.

The beast was insulted enough to stay quiet, but what he wasn't saying screamed as loud as a banshee.

What was happening to his body was not normal.

James's head was stuffed with cotton, though, and he just couldn't seem to remember *why* it wasn't normal.

He wrapped a hand around his cock, intending to ease off the pressure, but the first image that popped into his brain as he began to work himself was the last time he'd caught a glimpse of Kaylee stripping to shift…

He turned the temperature down on the shower and forced his hands away. Even with the temperature as low as it would go, the heat levels in his body continued to rise.

James gave up in frustration, dripping wet as he stomped through his bedroom. He pulled on jeans, grumbling loudly as he shoved his still-erect cock behind a zipper that threatened to tattoo itself along the rock-hard length.

He stomped to the living room and clicked on the TV for a distraction.

Bad idea.

"What the—?"

The oversized screen displayed two bodies writhing on a bed. Before James could blink, the woman had rolled on top, her ample upper body undulating, hips grinding over the man's groin as her long brown hair fell down her back, the splitting image of what Kaylee would look like if—

"Enough," he roared.

He stomped into the kitchen, ignoring the sound of his mother's voice in his head scolding that she was raising bears, not elephants.

Even though it was too early in the day to start drinking, he reached for a beer. He popped the top off and stood there with the door of the fridge open, cool air pouring over him as he tilted his head back and went to chug the contents.

A second later he whirled toward the sink and spewed,

liquid sloshing against the sides and dribbling down his chin.

"What the fuck?"

He eyed the beer then took a suspicious sniff.

Gagrhh.

Since when did alcohol go bad? But the liquid smelled horrible, and it tasted worse.

He upended the bottle into the sink and went for another one. This time he cracked the top more cautiously, taking a tiny sniff.

Bile rose in his throat. He flashed back to being about five years old, forced to eat a plate full of liver and lima beans.

Another bottle down the drain.

James rinsed the sink, then while the water was still running, he grabbed the moveable faucet head and pointed the cold water straight into his mouth, drinking thirstily. That at least, thank goodness, tasted fine.

Only, no matter how much he drank, it seemed his thirst wasn't quenched.

Kind of like last year, dumbass, his bear nudged him hard.

Shut—

James froze.

The water that had been aimed at his mouth misdirected, spraying all over his face and upper body, drenching the T-shirt he'd pulled on.

It'd taken a while, but it finally sank through his thick skull that this was no ordinary flu bug.

It was the mating fever.

He turned off the tap. Headed to the front door and checked the lock and security system. Each task done methodically and with great concentration before crossing the room to settle on the couch.

Silence fell. He leaned back on the soft leather and stared up at the ceiling.

Mating fever.

The grin that took him was huge and satisfying. *Finally*.

Finally, he could go after the woman he so desperately wanted to be his. Now she wouldn't be able to tell him he was simply playing around, not when he made it clear she was every answer to every question that had ever been asked.

If she wanted him a fraction of the amount he wanted her, this would be the beginning of a fan-fucking-tastic forever.

*D*amn bear.

Hours had passed, yet she was still daydreaming about James.

Kaylee had taken a roundabout trip to get outside, grabbing his clothing and tucking the pile away in her truck. Then she did as he'd suggested, snapping pictures around the outside of Borealis Gems before the weather turned.

It was over an hour later before she slipped back into the building and up to the office to track down her *other* best friend.

Amber Myawayan smiled at her from behind the executive assistant's desk in the main office. Her eyes shone, and she was all but quivering in her seat.

"What's got you so excited?" Kaylee asked.

"I found another lead on my brother," the ebony-haired woman told her, shaking a thin slip of paper in the air. Then her lips twisted, and she made a face, a sad sigh escaping before she added the confession. "It's not a very *good* lead, but it's better than nothing, and I've been waiting such a long time for a break. Maybe I'll actually find him this time."

Kaylee stepped toward her friend. Amber's deep brown eyes were so filled with hope, there was no way she could steal any of her joy. No matter that there had been nothing but dead ends at the end of each of Amber's searches ever since she had come north two years ago looking for her only remaining family.

"If there's anything I can do to help, let me know," Kaylee said with as much enthusiasm as possible.

"I know you don't want me to be disappointed again, but I have to keep hoping." Amber leaned toward Kaylee, her long hair falling forward as mischief danced in her eyes. "You have a secret too. Spit it out," she demanded.

For one panicked moment Kaylee wondered if she'd been talking about James out loud, then realized Amber was referring to the note she'd sent earlier in the day.

There were secrets, and there were *secrets*.

Her forever-crush on James was a private matter, but there'd been whispers on the air lately. Rumours trickling into Kaylee's ears that involved the Borealis family and a potential hostile takeover attempt of Borealis Gems.

Anything that might affect her family of choice wasn't going to remain hidden in the shadows. Not if she could help it.

Kaylee stepped toward the desk and lowered her voice. "I've been in contact with that certain person you thought would be good to talk to."

Her friend's eyes widened. "That certain person of the female persuasion who works for *you know who*?"

"At the *you know what*?" Kaylee dipped her chin. "She said she wants to meet with us."

Amber tilted her head to one side, looking every inch

like innocence personified. "Of course she does. Who wouldn't want to meet with two unintimidating, perfectly wonderful women such as ourselves?"

Kaylee's lips twitched into a smile no matter how hard she tried to stop them. "To say nothing about the fact you're hip-deep in contact with one of the most important people at Borealis Gems."

"*You're* hip deep," Amber corrected. A furl formed between her brows. "You and James have been friends forever. You know as well as I do that if you told him you had important news, he'd be willing to listen. I'm fairly new on the scene, and I just work for the company. They might not believe me."

Kaylee didn't know about that. Amber was the type most people trusted from the very first moment. Her, on the other hand, people were more likely to take one look and forget she even existed. Most of the time that was just fine.

Except...damn if she didn't wish it *wasn't* true because then, maybe then, she'd have been worthy of being more than a friend to James. More hands-on, specifically.

Or body on body. *Oh yeah...*

The door off the hallway opened, and they both snapped upright—in Kaylee's case, because of her guilty conscience from daydreaming dirty thoughts about her best friend while in the main office of the family company.

Relief hit as she recognized the man marching through the door. His bright eyes snapped with intelligence, the silver grey in his hair only enhancing his good looks. Giles Borealis, Sr. strutted forward as if he owned the place—*he literally did*—one hand resting on a cane Kaylee was convinced was more for show than anything else.

A debonair man of his age looked good with a cane by

his side, but she wasn't about to proclaim that the patriarch of Borealis Gems was playacting.

Although he totally was, and she knew it.

"Well, now, if it isn't two of the most beautiful women in the world. Breaks my heart, just the sight of you. Speeds up my pulse and makes a man wish he were twenty-five years younger."

Amber slid behind her desk as if putting a barrier between her and the older gentleman. She fussed with her notepad and phone, her eyes not meeting his, only Kaylee caught her friend's smile. The one she was trying to keep hidden from the family patriarch. "Wouldn't your wife have something to say about that?"

Giles Borealis made a pooh-poohing sound. "Oh, you can be sure that I would still fall in love with my Laureen, but I'd be most happy to have introduced you to some of my younger self's *friends*. Wonderful gentlemen who would treat you ladies to a good time instead of leaving you stuck in this office all the time." He shook a finger at Amber, who had settled in her chair and was now smiling at him sweetly. "I know you've got an important job, with a lot on your plate, but that's no excuse for you to stay home every night."

One of Amber's brows arched skyward. "How would you know where I spend my nights?"

A snort of laughter escaped Kaylee before she could stop it.

Bad move. Mr. Borealis turned his formidable attention on her. "And you," he said, ignoring Amber's question. "Why don't I see you settling down with some fine young man? It's time you made a move, young lady. You're beautiful and you're talented." He pointed to the family portrait that hung on the wall behind him, the one Kaylee had taken during a family picnic two years ago. He tapped his nail on the glass. "You give me the go-ahead, and I'll bankroll the loan to set you up with your own photo studio."

"Mr. Borealis, you can't just—"

He shook that finger in front of her face, gaze locked on hers, although he didn't say a word.

This one is entertaining, her cat muttered softly. *More feline than any bear should be.*

Kaylee couldn't argue. There was something very cat-like about the man's curiosity—and he was stubborn.

He'd corrected her on this far too many times in the past. "*Grandpa* Giles. You can't just up and offer that kind of business arrangement."

"As if I can't," he harrumphed. "I know a good investment when I see one. Your work is going to take you places, and anyone who blames a man for getting in on the ground floor doesn't have any business sense at all." He folded his arms over his chest and dipped his head as if that were the end of the conversation. His gaze slid back to Amber. "I came in to pick up the signed paperwork from the boys."

Amber's lashes fluttered for a moment. "Oh, dear. It's not ready. I mean, Cooper and Alex both signed, but James isn't home yet from—"

Drat.

"James is back," Kaylee interrupted. "But he headed straight home. I'm sorry, I was supposed to tell you."

Grandpa Giles clicked his tongue, worry erasing his happy expression. "I need those papers. I'm meeting virtually with the investors in a little over an hour, and I definitely need all the signatures in place."

Amber bit her bottom lip, obviously flustered as she rearranged and straightened papers on her desk. "I have an appointment later today. I've been invited to go to the dog sledding place. You know, the one where they run with teams over the grass? I don't want to cancel, but if I have to..."

"No. Don't worry about it. I can help," Kaylee offered.

The change in Grandpa Giles was astonishing. The sadness in his eyes vanished between one second and the next. He straightened up and looked her over with approval. "Would you really? Oh, you have no idea how big of a help that would be. I can keep the investors entertained during our conference call if you get James's signature quick enough."

While some things were beyond her skill set, this she was more than capable of. "It's not a problem. I wanted to make sure he was taking care of himself, anyway."

Curiosity and concern darkened Grandpa Giles's eyes. "Not feeling well?"

"He thinks he caught a cold from the group of investors he flew home. Either that, or it's the bug that's going around town."

Grandpa Giles nodded slowly. "Dangerous things, summer colds. And I know my grandsons—always neglecting their health. Good thing you're going to drop in on him. Someone needs to double check he's taking care of himself and getting lots of rest."

Amber had been working diligently in the background. She slid papers into a file folder and handed it to Kaylee. "Page four. Once he signs it, take a picture and send it to me. I'll have time to take care of the rest before I head out for the sleds."

"Amazing women," Grandpa Giles offered up as if he were reciting a prayer, "the world would be a sadder place without you."

Kaylee exchanged a secret smile with Amber before grabbing the file and slipping from the room.

Outside, the blue skies had vanished behind a mass of clouds that were roiling in like high-speed time-lapse photography. The threat of the storm was no longer just a suggestion.

Her inner cat took one look overhead, shuddered, then vanished. Hiding from the coming rain with incredibly self-centered preservation skills.

Thanks for nothing, Kaylee muttered.

A faint echo answered her, mostly prim, but with a faint hint of apology. *You chose to go outside. You chose to get wet, not* me.

True. But some things had to be faced and not hidden away from.

Kaylee clutched the file and raced for her truck.

In spite of her terrible history with inclement weather, as the first huge droplets smashed against her windshield on the short trip over to James's apartment, it wasn't fear that made her heart pound erratically.

Somehow it felt as if her world was on the edge of tumbling into something new. Something massive and earthshaking.

She parked in the nearest parking space to the door. No one else lived in the apartment building yet, which meant she was only a few feet from the entrance. Kaylee pushed open her door, barely catching it in time as the howling wind ripped in to tear it from her grasp. Her hair was instantly drenched, rain slashing against her skin. The fabric of her coat and her hair flailed like out-of-control whips.

Storms had terrified her ever since she'd been caught in one at age ten, when her parents had carelessly locked her

VIVIAN AREND

out of the house when they went exploring without any warning.

Her cat had hated every minute of the situation. They'd been wet and cold and scared, and only her inner animal had given her the strength to deal with just how petrified she'd been.

Come to think of it, that was probably the last time the beast had being willing to deal with that kind of stress, and Kaylee didn't blame her.

Yet the tingling in her entire body had nothing to do with the memories of spending that long-ago storm hiding all alone in a shaking and unsteady treehouse, and everything to do with putting her thumb to the security lock James had given her access to only a couple of weeks ago. Had everything to do with her dripping her way to the elevator and hitting the button to the penthouse suite.

Because as foolish as it was, her heart kept hoping for what could never be.

4

---

*H*eat. Pulsing heat. It wrapped around his body and tangled tentacles into his brain, sending his thoughts in a million directions.

James sat on his couch and died a million deaths. He'd reached for the phone a half dozen times before letting his hand fall with a plop to the leather seat beside him. It had to have something to do with the fever, his lack of ability to concentrate enough to make the next move. Who was he going to call, and what would he tell them?

His brothers? Hell, they'd laugh right before they reminded him that more was on the line than just his freedom—and reminded him of their pact.

No avoiding the mating fever. Well, he didn't plan to avoid it, but damn if he knew what he was supposed to do next.

He needed Kaylee to show up so he could get started on his grand master plan of thumbing his nose at fate and picking his own mate, but seriously, what was he supposed to say to her?

Kaylee? Hey, hi. Seems as if the mating fever might have

hit, and I was just wondering if you'd be interested in coming over here so I can have my wicked way with you. Possibly forever.

Yeah. Considering her previous response to his flirting, an outright demand would go over really well.

At this stage of the game, he still knew what was going on. His brain was still working, although his more primal side was beginning to take over, and at the height of the fever, at least according to rumours he'd heard, the animal urges would have the upper hand.

In a good, positive way in terms of sex drive. Again, rumours, because his own memories of last year were hazy.

He'd had the good luck of being off in the wilderness on a fishing trip by himself when the fever hit. He basically survived by shifting into his bear form and sitting in the river for most of the week.

Wasn't fun, his bear reminded him.

This isn't going to be, either, he informed the beast. Not if he couldn't get Kaylee on board quickly.

His inner animal pouted before offering a brilliant suggestion. *Call Kaylee. You can have sex. Lots and lots of sex. Would be fun.*

It would be. This time he agreed completely with the beast.

A rapid knocking at the door broke into his brooding.

He blinked, surprised to find the room had gone dark even though it was barely five. Rain slammed into the windows lining the side of the penthouse, a strong wind rattling even the solid construction of his multimillion-dollar home on the tenth-floor penthouse suite.

He leaned forward, peeling off the couch with a rasp as if he'd begun to melt his way into the leather surface.

The banging grew loud, irritating his nerves. He had the

urge to bang on his side of the door. See how *they* liked it when someone else made such an annoying racket.

"What?" he shouted bad-naturedly.

"It's me, Kaylee. Open the door. I'm freezing to death."

He'd already had his hands on the locks, twisting and opening, but at the sound of her voice, he went still. Except for his cock—the damned thing jerked upright behind the tight confines of his jeans, signaling its willingness to leap into action.

This was it. This was what he'd been hoping for all along, and yet he hesitated. Not with him already partially naked and his cock primed like a heat-seeking missile.

The image of his cock sliding into Kaylee's warm depths dragged a groan of frustration out of him loud enough to rattle the walls.

The knocking stopped, and the worry in Kaylee's voice became clear. "James. What's wrong? Are you hurt?"

The fact she sounded scared to death was the only reason he could do it. He undid the final dead bolt and pulled the door toward himself. No more than an inch, though, with his foot jammed against the bottom as if that was going to be enough to barricade her on the outside until he got in control of himself.

"I'm sick, remember?" he growled.

Maybe if he was a grumpy bastard she'd get mad and shout loud enough to kill his boner.

He was greeted by a sight that had him pulling the door all the way open instantly. Kaylee was soaked from head to toe, her T-shirt plastered against her skin. Her hair lay in soggy ringlets over her face and her warm copper-coloured skin had paled to an unhealthy grey.

She shivered hard enough *his* teeth rattled, but still she

held forward a rain-drenched file folder. "You n-n-need to s-s-sign these p-p-papers."

Her entire body wavered, barely keeping vertical.

Fuck. Fuckity, fuck, *fuck*.

James put his teeth together carefully so he didn't bite off his tongue, then he scooped her up his arms and carried her into the apartment.

Oh my God. Soft skin, icy cool, lay under his fingers, the weight of her body pressed close to him. Her breath was warm against his neck as she turned her face toward him and cuddled in.

James began to swear silently. Alphabetically. Creatively.

He grabbed the file from her fingers, dropping it on the table they passed as he marched straight into the bathroom. He got her feet to the ground by shaking her free and turning on the water. He was gentleman enough to block the spray of cold water with his back, but the instant it warmed up, he stepped aside.

"Stay there," he ordered.

He turned to move away—and froze. The most curious sensation had just slid over his skin. The closest thing he could compare it to was as if they were two pieces of Velcro and he'd actually had to undo the connection between them one section at a time to be able to step away.

Weird.

Ignoring the strange tugging, he marched determinedly to his dresser.

He had every intention of following through and making Kaylee his, but damn if he was going to be an animal about it.

Am animal, his bear reminded him. *Partly.*

Shut up.

Just saying...

Dry jeans. Dry socks. James grabbed a T-shirt and pulled it on. Then a sweatshirt, then a hoodie—just in case extra layers between them would act as a deterrent. If his winter clothes hadn't been in storage, he would've hauled on a parka.

Only once he was dressed in layers of veritable armour did he dare to go back into the bathroom.

Kaylee had stripped off her wet things and put them in the sink. Her arms were wrapped around her body, and she stood directly under the showerhead. Her face was tilted up, presented to the falling water as if she were a nymph worshipping the rain gods. Her wet hair lay in curly strands over her shoulders, rivulets of water curling down her body and over her skin.

He didn't know if he should curse or bless the steam that had produced a foggy surface on the glass shower wall, leaving him with shadowy images instead of clear, lust-inducing perfection.

But damn if he could turn his eyes away. "What's in the file?"

Kaylee jerked her hands up to cover herself, head swiveling toward him, eyes wide with panic.

He deliberately twisted until his back was to her, offering privacy.

Only, bastard that he was, he could see her reflection in the shaving mirror on the countertop.

The good part about being a masochistic asshole was that peeking meant he saw the tension go out of her, her shoulders relaxing. "Papers they need your signature on as soon as possible. I promised I'd get it to you then email a photo back to Amber at the office."

"I'll take care of it," he grumbled then escaped the room.

Once again that strange peeling sensation struck as he moved away, stronger this time. He forced his concentration onto the paperwork before tossing it in the scanner and sending it to work.

Now there was only her and him and the fever.

After Kaylee was warmed up and out of the shower, he'd loan her dry clothes. Then they'd sit in the living room like rational adults and talk about the future.

No. Better idea, his bear suggested. *Not feeling well. Should go to bed.*

It was brilliant. It was perfect. He was actually a little surprised his bear had come up with it. Of course. She'd be dressed, he'd be under the covers. That would give them lots of room to discuss facts.

He stripped off all the layers he had on—*why the hell was he wearing a sweater* and *a hoodie?*—and crawled into bed naked. He tugged the light quilt over his big frame and tried to get into the perfect position so there was room for Kaylee to sit beside him and talk when she was ready.

Like friends. Like old friends who cared a lot about each other.

Like old friends who were going to fuck each other's brains out all week long.

Happy sigh.

He lay there with his eyes half closed, trying to get into the spirit of it. Rearranging his body to reduce the pressure on his cock, which was all but throbbing with urgency.

The shower shut off. There was no stopping the images that popped into his mind. Kaylee grabbing a towel. Kaylee running the soft cotton all over her smooth skin, her breasts, between her legs.

He rolled slightly to give his cock extra room.

The door opened, near silent footfalls crossing into his room.

Close eyes, his bear suggested.

Brilliant, he told his bear.

He closed them, following Kaylee's movement by sound alone. A game of hide-and-seek just like when they were young. She'd never see him lying here so still. Not until the moment he was ready to spring out and surprise her.

His chest of drawers opened then closed. A pause, then Kaylee's footsteps slid toward the bed. Stopped.

She smelled—*oh my God,* she smelled delicious. He took a deep breath and let it out slowly, all but salivating at the taste of her in the air.

She stepped closer.

He cracked one eye open.

That—that one single moment—was his downfall.

Kaylee had a towel wrapped around her head, and she'd grabbed one of his T-shirts from the drawer and slipped it on. The light from the hallway shone through the worn fabric and silhouetted her perfect body as she turned. All curves and dips and luscious woman.

The part of his brain that would normally have told him to stay in control sizzled out with the heat burning through him.

He opened both eyes and a low growl escaped. Kaylee twirled on the spot, the shirt rising briefly to reveal more of her long legs, and he was helpless to resist.

James flashed out a hand and caught hold of her wrist, trapping her in place.

5

*D*amn bear.

She'd been ninety-nine percent sure James had fallen asleep. His arm shooting out so suddenly sent her heart racing, but as she settled on the mattress beside him and laid her free hand against his forehead, her concern brushed her temporary panic away.

He was burning up.

"Poor baby. You're in a bad way. Don't worry," she assured him as soothingly as possible, stroking the hair off his forehead. "I'll take care of you."

"Promise?" he whispered.

"Of course," she whispered back. His head must ache. She let her fingers drift down his cheek, the layer of dark stubble making her palm tingle.

"I know what I need," James muttered, deep and dark. The rumble of his voice stroked her skin.

"Juice?" she offered. "Tylenol?"

With one quick tug, he toppled her off balance.

Kaylee bit back a scream as she thrust out her arms to

stop her momentum. She ended up with one arm on either side of his body, the towel on her head staying mostly in place except for sliding slightly over one eye. It had only taken a second for her to end up fully stretched out over his hard torso, heat blasting upward as if she'd landed on a sun-scorched rock.

Hmmmm. I like. Her inner kitty had no trouble voicing approval.

Kaylee? Felt turned on and guilty at the same time.

He'd released her wrist only to jam one hand against her lower back, pinning their bodies together. The other hand wrapped around the back of her neck, tight enough to control, soft enough to caress.

Hard muscular body under her, hard length of his co—

Oh my God, his cock pressed against her torso. Impossibly hard. Impossibly thick.

Well, that's impressive, her cat observed drily.

Hush, I'm in the middle of something, Kaylee warned.

His eyes glinted as if he'd heard her internal dialogue. "What I need..." he began as if they were sitting at the kitchen table deciding what to order for dinner takeout, "is simple."

She wiggled, stopping instantly. Changing position rubbed her over all the hard things she was lying on, and that was probably dangerous. "James, sweetie. You need to let me up."

"No, I need you down," he stated clearly.

Kaylee opened her mouth but had to close it. "Nope. Sorry, but you're too feverish to understand."

He rolled until she was under him, the quilt flying off the bed in the process. His elbows braced on either side of her, hips pressed between her thighs. Her legs had fallen open, and he fit perfectly against her, like a puzzle piece where all the knobs and holes lined up.

And wasn't that thought going to make future puzzle-solving far too kinky to do in mixed company...

James lowered his head and nuzzled his scratchy cheek against hers.

"Hmmm," he murmured. "You smell good."

"*James.*" She said his name firmly, in case volume would get through the cotton in his brain. "You need to stop."

She slipped her hands over his shoulders, intending to push him away, but the instant she touched naked skin, a pulse of need shot deep. As if a current had run from her palms, up her arms and streaked as quickly as possible to tag her clit with high-voltage impact.

Kaylee gasped, then lost the air as he rocked his hips. Pressure slid over sensitive places and made her skin tingle everywhere.

Maybe *she* was the one who was feverish. That was it—she'd gotten lost on the way to James's place and they'd found her rain-soaked body days later. She was now in a coma.

A sex coma, from all the clues, and waking up was going to be very sad.

Please. You're being overly dramatic, her cat drawled.

I'm busy, Kaylee reminded her sharply.

He pulled back just far enough to meet her gaze. "I'm going to kiss you," he warned.

"Hey, if you're all germ-laden and stuf—"

He stole her protest. Softly, with a mere brush of his lips over hers. Back and forth slowly, until every breath took extra energy to suck in, push out.

What the hell? People in sex comas couldn't be held

42

responsible for their misguided actions. She locked her fingers in his hair and kissed him back.

Gentleness vanished. The instant she moved toward him, James consumed her. His tongue slid along hers then took possession. His weight pinned her in place, his fingers guiding her head to exactly the right position so he could ravish her mouth.

It was heat and passion and wonderful. Kaylee was melting into the mattress as his body meshed with hers and fire raced up her spine. Her mind was going numb as all parts of her body lit up with need.

When he finally broke away from her lips, it was to kiss and bite and lick his way along her jaw. Under her ear —*massive shiver*—and down her neck.

"James. Stop," she whispered.

Shockingly, he did. Absolute stillness hit between one breath and the next, his mouth still touching her skin.

Her pulse was shoving blood through her system hard enough she was surprised the walls weren't echoing back the beat.

This...this...*thing* happening between them was not normal. It was amazing, and incredible, and oh so tempting, but...

A memory scratched its way through her lustful haze, nearly back to the surface. "James. What's going on?"

"I need you," he moaned, his lips brushing her skin and making goose bumps rise.

"Of course you do. You're sick, I'm your friend—"

"Want you as my lover. Always have, and now I can keep you."

Great. He was so feverish he was delusional. It was tough to say the words, but she made herself tell the truth. "We're not lovers, dude. We're good, *good* friends who shouldn't be lying tangled up with each other. You're going to regret this in the morning."

"Never regret. Want to pick, not have fate decide. Want you for always. Want you as my mate."

Mate—

Did he say mate? her cat murmured. *How...unexpected.*

Shit. Understanding slipped in between one aching pulse and the next. No one who'd spent any time around polar bear shifters was unaware of the mating fever and all its consequences.

Oh no. Oh no, no, *no.* Because as much as she'd had a lustful, long-term crush on the man, there was no way in hell she was letting him make a mistake like this.

Kaylee tightened her grip on his hair and jerked her hands. Hard.

She pulled out a chunk of his hair, and he budged all of three inches. It was far enough to look him in the eye. "James. Buddy. Pal o' mine. Do you have the mating fever?"

His lips were lifted in a delicious smile. His gaze dropped to stare at her as if she were dessert and he'd been a very good boy. "I have you. You're in my arms. I'm going to make love to you all night long, and then in the morning, I'm going to start again, and I'm never going to stop. Never, not even when we're old. Even then I'll tell you all the dirty things I want to do to you, and we'll always be together."

Yeah. Awesome. Definitely mating fever.

Kaylee patted his cheek gently. "Right. So, maybe it's not a good idea I'm here right now. Since you're mating feverish and all, and I'm not a very good person to be your mate."

"Perfect person." He frowned, growling low. "Kaylee perfect."

His bear was in his eyes. *Shit.*

44

She caressed him again, attempting to soothe the beast. "Okay, big guy. I need to..." *Think. Think, Kaylee.* "I need to do something first. Okay? You need to go have a shower, and I need to get the thing from the thing."

Confusion twisted his face. "Really?"

"Uh-huh." She nodded, scratching his shoulder.

The bear looked back at her.

"You go shower," she whispered. "I'll be right back."

His reluctance to leave was obvious, but she kept smiling and nodding encouragingly. "I need a shower?"

She didn't remember hearing that mating fever made guys stupid, but hey, she had to play with the hand they'd been dealt. "Shower. While I get the thing."

For one split second she thought she was a goner. He rocked against her slowly, hard muscles and smooth skin teasing her to the edge of sanity.

But then he rose, staring at her with dark bear eyes as he brought her to her feet beside him. He bent slightly and lifted her chin. "I'm going to take a shower, and when I get back, you're mine."

Kaylee wasn't ready for the kiss he planted on her. For the heat and the urgency, and the way her entire body ached and begged her to follow him into the shower and let him do his worst.

But when he stepped back, ragged breaths shaking his chest, his eyes bright with fever, she knew she had to do the right thing.

The instant he entered the bathroom, she moved. She yanked the towel off her head, bunched her hair into a knot and fixed it in place with an elastic band she found on the dresser.

She grabbed her wet shoes and the clothes she'd hung over chairs to dry, then raced down the hallway, pausing just long enough to put on the shoes and slip the rest of her things into a bag she found on the kitchen counter.

Outside the window, the storm was in full swing.

Seriously? Warm apartment, warm man, and you want us to go out there? Her cat was indignant.

We can't stay, Kaylee insisted.

Her cat all but pouted, then once again vanished.

Kaylee shuddered but forced herself to keep moving. She snatched up the soft throw blanket off the couch and wrapped it around her shoulders as a coat, then left the apartment at a near run.

Waiting for the elevator was torture. What if he figured out she was running away? What if she couldn't get away in time to save him from making the biggest mistake of his life?

The wind outside had to be gale-force level. It shrieked up the elevator shaft, creating a whistling sound like nails on a blackboard.

The doors slid open, and Kaylee rushed forward, hitting the button for the ground floor and then stabbing the *close door* button repeatedly. She held her breath as she stared at the apartment door, willing the elevator to shut on time.

Hurry, hurry, hurry.

The massive metal sheets finally moved, sliding together in three, two, one...

Kaylee sighed in relief. Once she was a safe distance away, she would phone James. They would have a rational conversation about why, even though she liked him plenty and they would always be friends, she would be a terrible mate.

Taking fate into his own hands? That's not how this worked.

A sudden crackle rang out followed by an echoing metallic *boom*, as if someone had dropped a bowling ball down a laundry chute. Blue light oozed through the narrow line between the doors in front of her, and the smell on the air was ozone and charcoal.

The elevator jerked to a stop.

The lights went out.

6

*J*ames was two steps from the shower when something registered as wrong. The itch in his brain escalated.

Why was he taking a shower now? He'd had one earlier in the day, when he got home from his trip.

He marched back into his bedroom and looked around in confusion. There was something he was supposed to do...

Be doing...?

Nope. Couldn't figure it out.

He strode toward the living room and nearly tripped over a sodden pair of jeans abandoned on the floor. He lifted them in the air in confusion. Sniffed. A familiar scent filled his nostrils.

Why was there a pair of Kaylee's pants—

Kaylee? In his apartment.

Without pants.

He marched quickly through the suite, but she clearly wasn't in his bedroom, nor the living room or kitchen. James ignored the rain pounding against the window and pushed out onto the balcony. He hung over the railing far enough to check the visitor parking.

Spotting Kaylee's dump of a truck didn't make the big picture any clearer.

He had just straightened up when a lightning bolt shot across the sky like in a comic strip panel. The jagged white line blasted from the storm-blackened clouds directly toward his apartment. The roar of thunder arrived at the same moment as the lightning, shaking the windows, deafeningly loud in his ears.

An instant later, he was flying through the air before slamming into the concrete wall behind him.

For a moment, all James could see were stars floating in front of his eyes. Everything else had gone pitch-black, and his ears rang.

The scent of burnt hair made his nose crinkle in disgust, and he raised his hands in front of his face to discover his vison clearing on the sight of curled and shriveled hair on his knuckles in the few spots it wasn't fried away.

Well, that'd been freaking exciting. He'd never been struck by lightning before. He got to his feet and shook his head to settle his brains back into place. Nope, electrocution wasn't a thrill he was looking to repeat any time soon.

He'd just closed the balcony doors behind him when three things hit simultaneously.

The scent of Kaylee in his suite, recent and crisp.

An urgent ache in his gut that said he needed to find her, *now*.

The clear sound of his cell phone going off with Cooper's ringtone.

The clothes he'd worn out on his last trip were on his dining room table, sort of in a pile, with his cell phone on top. Even as James answered the call, the memories of the past hours slipped neatly into place, although he wasn't sure what had screwed them up to start with.

Holy shit, this had been the weirdest day yet, and it was far from over. Phone call, then he was tracking down his mate.

"What?" James demanded. "I'm kind of in a hurry."

"You're in trouble, that's what you are," Cooper drawled. "How're you feeling?"

James marched to his bedroom to get dressed so he could go track down Kaylee and fix what he'd broken between them as soon as possible. Not to mention so he could fuck her silly and take her as a mate. "Annoyed. My brother insists on talking to me when I'm in the throes of mating fever, and my woman just vanished for some goddamned reason. Oh, and the power is out. Oh, and I got hit by lightning. *Annoyed* pretty much covers it, though."

The dead silence on the other end of the line was unexpected.

"Talk or I'm hanging up," James ordered.

"I'm shocked to find you this coherent," Cooper confessed, his words coming out sharp and crisp. Accelerating as if he was reading his brother's mind and getting to the point before James followed through on his threat. "Kaylee called Amber who called me. Seems Kaylee's stuck in your elevator, and she's worried because you've got the mating fever and are insistent you want her as your mate."

"I do want her as my mate. Damn it, the elevator? Power surge must have fried out the entire building when the lightning struck. I'll have to climb down to save her," James said in a hurry. "You'll have to contact emergency services to make sure there's no one else in the building who needs help. And get my power up and running ASAP, got it?"

"Wait," Cooper said sharply. "How come you're not stupid with the fever right now? This is only your second time—it took years before I wasn't mindless the entire seven days I was feverish. Are you sure you've got it?"

The desperate need to be with Kaylee was growing stronger by the minute, and his skin was on fire, but thankfully his mind was crystal clear. "Maybe getting struck by lightning cured the stupid—and why the hell didn't you or Alex warn me about that part? Assholes."

"Rite of passage. But slow down. Kaylee was scared to call you for help. Maybe I should come—"

A full-fledged roar escaped James's throat at the thought of another unmated male near his Kaylee.

"—and forget I even mentioned it," Cooper added smoothly. "You sure you know what you're doing?"

James snorted. "Absolutely. Lightning strikes are great for clearing the confusion. I think I even know why she didn't call me for help, but don't worry. Everything will be fine. She's mine. We belong together."

He didn't wait for Cooper to say goodbye. Just stabbed the *off* button and finished yanking on his clothes.

Kaylee obviously had a working phone, but calling her to say he was on his way wasn't going to get her rescued any sooner. He shoved emergency supplies into a bag, pulled on his coat, and made his way to the elevator control station.

Thank goodness Alex, in his role of head of security, had insisted all family members knew the inner workings of all potential escape routes from their buildings.

Of course, his brother had been raving about espionage and kidnappings and other impossible scenarios at the time, but the end result was James knew exactly which panels to remove to get access to the support cables for the stuck elevator.

He shined his flashlight into the darkness then checked the master controls.

"Damn it."

The elevator cage was caught between floors. There was no easy way to get Kaylee in or out without joining her.

First things first, then—and at least being trapped together would give them time to talk where she couldn't run away.

James slipped on the leather gloves he found on the work shelf by the controls, slung his bag over his shoulder, and got ready to make a move.

Maybe a warning was in order...

"Hey, Kaylee."

Even from a lot of floors away he heard her gasp. Words followed, albeit muffled. "James? No, you need to stay away."

"I need to be with you, Kaylee Kat. Don't worry. I'm in my right mind this time." He caught the thick cable in both hands. "I'll be landing on the roof of the elevator in a minute. Expect a bang, okay? It's just me."

"I'm scared." The confession came out softly. "So scared."

"I'll make it better," he promised before wrapping his teeth around his flashlight and making the jump.

The slide downward would have been exhilarating if this weren't a rescue mission. James moved quickly but tried to land as softly as possible to keep from rocking Kaylee. Poor woman was worried enough.

His feet touched down, and he quickly took the light from his mouth, unscrewing the ceiling access as he spoke. "I'm here. You're safe."

He lifted the escape panel out of the way and poked his head into the black box that held his woman trapped.

Kaylee was curled up in the corner, wrapped in one of his throw blankets. She held her phone in front of her like a candle, the golden light from the screen reflecting off her face.

Her worried and tear-streaked face. At the sight of her fear and sadness, his gut dropped five feet. "Oh, sugar, it's okay. It's all going to be okay."

She shook her head. "I'm so sorry."

James forced himself to chuckle as if he didn't have a care in the world. "Nothing to be sorry about. Let me drop the things I brought, and I'll be right with you."

Because once he got her into his arms, he wasn't going to let her go.

7

———

*I*t had taken her minutes, not seconds, to react after being plunged into darkness.

She'd actually had to close her eyes and pretend she was just sitting in her room to be able to stop shaking enough to grab her phone and call for help.

Her inner cat was no help—not only was the creature mad at having left the warm apartment, her cat disliked dark places just as much as Kaylee did.

Although the beast would never admit it.

And now, as James dropped toward her, sadness enveloped her harder than the terror that had shaken her in the dark.

She hadn't been able to save him.

Maybe if she was really, really lucky she could find a way to hold him off, but with them trapped together in close quarters, it was a long shot, considering what she'd heard about the mating fever.

Considering how he'd been acting before she escaped his apartment.

His feet touched down and the elevator shifted. Kaylee

squeezed her eyes together and bit her jaw down to keep from crying out.

Then she was being scooped up in his arms, cradled against his body.

"I'm sorry for scaring you earlier," he murmured. James put his back to the wall and slid downward. She ended up in his lap, legs draped over his.

He wrapped a hand around the back of her head and tugged her to his chest, then rearranged the blanket over the two of them and just held her.

After being terrified that the elevator was going to plummet to the ground, this moment of being protected was exactly what she needed. His heartbeat rang firmly under her ear, and his breathing evened out. She tried to keep pace and found herself relaxing in the darkness, guarded by the big bear shifter who'd been her friend forever.

The one about to make a terrible mistake. *Oh dear*.

"Hey," he soothed, rubbing her back in circles. "It's okay."

She couldn't keep the tension from returning. "It's not okay, on so many levels."

"Well, since we don't really have anywhere to go for the next while, maybe we should talk about all the things that have you tensing up like a bowstring."

"You're going to be stubborn about this, aren't you?" she complained.

"Stubborn as a bear," he teased back.

The phrase was familiar and so theirs that Kaylee pushed away from him. She hauled out her phone and turned on the screen so she could see his face.

He was smiling. Or at least his lips were curled upward, but there was a hint of sadness in his eyes that made her heart ache. "Why are you looking at me like that?" she asked sincerely.

"Because I'm glad to be here with you, but I'm sorry I scared you away. We could be enjoying the blackout in the safety of my suite right now."

"Staying with you wasn't a good idea," she said drolly. And sitting on him wasn't too smart, either. He didn't seem to be acting weird anymore, but he was still fiery hot.

Surely he couldn't just turn off the mating fever?

Kaylee wiggled with the intention of moving to her own corner of the space.

Nope. His arms locked tighter. "Stay where you are. You're cold, and we can talk with you sitting where you are just as easily as with you freezing all by your lonesome."

She growled at him in frustration. "Bossy bastard."

"You ain't seen nothing, Banks. Now let's go through your bullshit list of what's currently not okay in your world, shall we?"

Bullshit list? She tilted her phone to shine at her face so he could see her glare of disapproval.

James snorted.

Fine. He was going to be an asshole when she'd been trying to save him from himself? "We're trapped in an elevator, and it could fall and kill us any moment."

"We're currently locked in place by the best backup system my overbearing oldest brother could purchase," he countered. "Cooper paid extra to have emergency double redundancy systems in place for exactly this kind of circumstance."

She pondered that, blinking when James snorted in obvious amusement.

"I still think my idea of a backup power source would

have been even handier, but that'll be an argument for the next time I see him."

Oh. "So, we're safe?"

"Safe and sound. But trapped, at least until Cooper finds a way to turn the power back on."

At least she could put dying off her list of concerns.

The rest of it—

She took a deep breath and blurted it all out.

"You have mating fever, or you did, and you were raving about wanting me for a mate. And you can't. I mean, you're my best friend, and I like you tons. I do think you're attractive, sexy even, but there's no way you can be with me forever. You're...*you*. I'm...*me*. I'd be terrible for you as a mate."

He rubbed his chin against the top of her head and hummed happily. "You think I'm sexy?"

Arghhh. "*That's* all you pulled out of my confession?" she snapped.

"Other than the bit about me being your best friend, it was the only part worth listening to."

Oh. Hell. No.

She grabbed hold of the front of his shirt with both hands and shook him. She had to make him understand. "I'm scared to death of so many things, and you're the public face of your family's company. I can't talk to strangers. I can't go to business meetings in all parts of the world because I'm scared to fly. I would *die* if I had to get up beside you on a stage and schmooze with people."

"Is that what's got your knickers in a twist?"

A small scream escaped as she rose in the darkness. James had caught hold of her, lifting and twisting so when she landed, she was straddling him.

His hand reclaimed her neck. The other landed low on her body, keeping her from being able to squirm away.

"Let's see if I can answer the rest of your worries. Yes, I have the mating fever, and yes, I was raving—sorry about that. You can hit Alex and Cooper later for not warning us that the first years of fever tend toward bear-in-charge stupidity."

Okay, that made sense. "I saw your bear in your eyes —*wait*. You still have the fever?"

He ignored her and went on. "I'm apologizing for the raving bit, not the desire to have you as my mate. You're my best friend, Kaylee. And I like you tons, too. You're also sexy as fuck, and I can't think of anything I want more than to have you beside me forever."

"You're not listening," she shouted. Although the *sexy as fuck* part had been nice to hear. "I'd be *terrible* for you."

"This isn't a job application," he stated back, louder than before, but not yet reaching her volume. "I'm not looking for a publicity partner. I'm looking for a mate."

She didn't see it coming. Literally, since it was completely dark and they'd been having the entire conversation in a small seven-by-seven-foot metal box that caused their words to echo off the walls.

He caught her with her mouth open, kissing her with heat and wetness, tongue and teeth. That hand on her lower back tugged her in tighter until the entire front of their bodies connected.

The fear that had rushed her earlier was swallowed up whole by the greedy way he took her mouth. The worry he was making a terrible choice was consumed by the ardour roaring between their bodies.

Everything that was wrong was shoved to the side by

the lust that had been denied for far too long. It lit every nerve in her body and sent her reeling.

She'd tried to stop him. She'd failed. Now it was up to fate.

Kaylee slid her fingers into his thick hair and fisted tight. Holding his lips to hers so she could give back as good as she got. His tongue slicked over hers, and she moaned.

No longer cold, alone, or fearful, she was the one who came out the winner in this deal.

Even that thought made her sad.

James disconnected their lips, breath escaping in pants as he fought for control. He leaned his forehead against hers, speaking softly. "You're perfect the way you are. I swear."

"It's just—"

"*Kaylee.*"

She took a deep breath. "I don't want to hurt you," she whispered.

He kissed her gently. "Then don't run away or abandon me again. That's the only thing you could do that would hurt."

It was a reasonable request. "I'm sorry."

"Forgiven. Promise me you'll talk to me if you get worried, just like we've always talked about everything."

She snorted. "Obviously that's not true."

His confusion hovered on the air even as he stroked his fingers over the back of her neck. Caressing. Teasing. "What have we not talked about?"

It was easy to smile in the darkness where he couldn't see it. "'Sexy as fuck'? I had no idea."

A low chuckle escaped him. "Ditto. But I'm glad you feel the same way. I want my mate willing to jump my bones."

"Jumping could be arranged," she whispered. She curled against his chest, trying to push aside the lingering worries he seemed so willing to dismiss. "But can I request we not do it for the first time in an elevator?"

"We might be here for a long time," he warned, "if they can't get the power restored. I might find it hard to resist the mating fever."

Kaylee had forgotten about that part—he was so much more in control now than he'd been before. "Are you in pain?"

"Some. You can make it better, though."

"Yeah?"

"I need a little to tide me over."

She paused in the middle of petting his chest sympathetically. "Need a little what?"

His lips brushed her ear. "You. Perfect, wonderful, *delicious* you."

8

*J*ames kicked his own butt for not figuring out earlier that all her protests were because Kaylee was trying to be noble and completely underestimating herself.

Utter bullshit—her not being perfect for him.

Even the way she snuggled in tight, her hands stroking him as if trying to ease his pain, was exactly what he needed.

Well, he needed a bit more, but he was enough in control that the mating fever was like an intriguing plot line in a favourite TV show. He could see the pivotal moment approaching, but in the meantime, it was fun to figure out exactly how they would get to doing the deed.

The beginning of forever. He didn't need to rush.

In fact, now that he was in his right mind, he realized he had a few options available to make this moment more than just an acceptance of the animal magnetism between them.

He drifted his fingers forward until he cupped her face. Pressing his lips to hers for a very gentle kiss. "Don't move."

It only took a moment to settle her to one side, carefully tugging the blanket around her shoulders to keep her warm.

A soft laugh escaped her lips, teasing his senses. "Gee, I was planning on doing a CrossFit workout."

James reached for the bag of supplies he'd brought with him, unzipping the front compartment and pulling out a set of flashlights. "If you're looking for exercise, I'm pretty sure I can get your heart rate going."

He clicked on the first light, adjusting it to a warm glow. He did the same with the second, then tucked them into the far corners of the elevator. The light reflected off the decorative mirrors and turned the small space into a cozily lit oasis.

James glanced at Kaylee to discover her eyes were wide open, her lips glistening as if she'd just licked them.

Oh, yeah, he could totally do something to get both their hearts pounding.

He reached into the bag and pulled out a bottle of water, passing it over. "Drink. I don't want you to get dehydrated."

The heat in her eyes gave way to amusement. "You just said we might be stuck in here for a while. If you give me too much to drink, this is not going to end well."

Good point, although she really didn't have anything to worry about.

"Trust me," he said softly. "Just a couple swallows." She'd cried out enough moisture that she really had to replace it.

Her shoulders lifted in a gentle shrug, obviously willing to put up with him being a bossy bastard. "Just believe me when I say there are some things I don't want to share."

It was his turn to laugh. When she handed the bottle back, he took it in one hand then relaxed against the wall opposite the lights. A second later, he pulled her on his lap so she was straddling him, taking the time to drape the blanket over her shoulders again.

Kaylee stared down, the gentle light revealing her worried expression. "What if I hurt you?" she asked again.

"You never will," he promised. "Now, considering we've been friends forever, maybe the easiest way to switch things up is to do this one step at a time."

"Go slowly. That makes sense." She swallowed. Dipped her chin. "Can I touch you?"

Oh, hell yeah. He reached over his head and grabbed his T-shirt, stripping it off and tossing it aside. "Be my guest."

Since this was supposed to be a slow seduction, he didn't insist she do the same. Instead, James waited as Kaylee placed her palms against his chest. Such a gentle touch as she began to explore, but every nerve was sensitized and alert. Anticipation built as she scratched her nails lightly, not even aware her breath had hitched a notch.

She stroked again, her eyes widening as a low growl he couldn't control rumbled up from deep inside.

He watched her. Breathed deep and took in as much of her scent as possible. Felt every tremor that stole up her body, leaving her fingers quivering.

James lowered his hands to her hips, gentle yet possessive. Anchoring himself, more to make sure he didn't grab her so tightly that he hurt her than anything else—

He'd regained his control, but it was a tenuous thing.

The edge of her T-shirt had ridden up and his thumbs brushed bare skin. As her palms drifted over his chest and shoulders, her gaze fixed on the point of contact between them, he tortured himself by sneaking his fingers against her. Skin-to-skin contact. The smallest bit.

She dragged her palm over the stubble on his chin, a small smile twisting her lips. "I can't believe this is happening."

Sadness still haunted her eyes, and he needed to do something, stat. Needed to get her to stop tormenting herself before the protective instincts inside him let the bear loose again.

"You're thinking too hard," he told her. "Let's do something about that."

He eased forward just enough that she had to move closer to meet his lips in the middle. When she did, it was him who felt the shudder rack his body. His skin came alive as he took her taste into his mouth, happiness and joy in the motion as if the lightness that was her soul was dancing on his taste buds.

He'd said she was perfect, and as the kiss deepened and Kaylee slid her hands over his shoulders and down his back, bumping their torsos together, he knew it was true. He'd never felt this before. Never felt this deeply or fully.

Sexual craving and the urgency to be inside her was like a white-hot coal in his gut, but the realization his best friend was smooching with him, with flashlights providing ambience, made him smile against her lips.

It was sexual but also fun. Just like them.

Their torsos were close enough her nipples poked against his chest, the hard tips blatantly obvious.

Kaylee twisted her head enough to break contact, dragging in a breath before letting it out in a soft sigh against his cheek. "Not thinking so good anymore," she informed him.

"More," he demanded.

She reconnected their lips, but at the same time, she

reached down and took hold of his wrists. The kissing was a nice distraction, but he hated letting go of her hips.

The tugging of her hands was too insistent to ignore. Still, James was about to grumble when Kaylee reached her destination, and his mental circuitry fried out.

She'd pressed his palms against her breasts.

"Goddamn it, Kaylee."

Even to his own ears his voice sounded one step shy of begging. He understood completely when Kaylee laughed. "I thought you said you wanted more."

Challenge fucking accepted.

He touched her, and she groaned in pleasure, head falling back as her fingers tightened, nails digging into his wrists.

He rolled his finger and thumb again, teasing her nipples like he'd done a moment earlier. "I did. So do you."

Her breathing picked up a notch, a pulse beating frantically at the base of her throat. The entire time James pinched and tugged, holding the heavy weight of one breast in his hand as he tormented the other.

The agenda said go slow, but it was impossible to not do the next thing. He shoved her T-shirt up, exposing her skin. It only took a second to jostle her into position to wrap his lips around the tight peak.

"James." His name was a moan of need.

Pulling off with a gentle pop, he licked the tip then blew across it.

Kaylee wiggled in his arms, rising up on her knees. Helping put herself into a position where he could play more easily.

Awesome. Like magic, her T-shirt was gone, and he had both hands and his mouth on her. Kaylee let out a squeal, clutching his head.

There might've been a bit of teeth involved this time.

"Oh, James. *Yes*..." The word echoed as she hissed in pleasure. He sucked again, hard enough to draw a gasp from her lips.

He could do this all day, and sometime, he would. But the way she was squirming over him said his woman needed something more than this playing, as delightful as it was.

He buried his face between her breasts and took a deep breath, catching hold of her hips again.

A little sound of need rose from the back of her throat.

"It's okay, Kaylee Kat. I'll take care of you." Another promise. One he was desperately looking forward to keeping.

He pressed her legs farther apart until she was spread wide over his thighs. Then he caught hold of her hips and dragged her closer. Watching as her eyes widened again and her mouth pulled into a small O of pleasure.

"Feel good?" he asked with a grin.

What came out of her mouth wasn't coherent, but it was understandable. He rocked her again, dragging the core of her sex over the lead pipe bulging in his jeans. When he leaned in just the slightest bit, their torsos rubbed as well, her nipples dragging over the hair on his chest.

Kaylee caught hold of his shoulders, biting down on her bottom lip as she joined in and rocked against him, helping drive their pleasure higher.

He took her lips, possessing her mouth greedily even as the pressure on his cock stole up the back of his spine. A tingling sensation that was familiar and yet brand-new. Her tongue tangled with his, her fingernails digging into his shoulders as she pulsed frantically, trying to reach the pinnacle.

He released one hip so he could bring his hand up to

her chest and catch hold of a breast again, squeezing one tight tip between his thumb and forefinger. His other hand pressed firmly against her lower back as he ground himself against her.

All finesse vanished. This was a frantic, wild motion between the two of them that was perfect and dirty and desperate.

Kaylee's head dropped back as a cry escaped her lips. Her body pulsed against him, heart racing loud enough to be a drumbeat in his ears.

He pulled back far enough to stare into her eyes, and that's what made him come. The carefree, absolute pleasure on the face of the woman he wanted to be his forever.

9

*K*isses brushed across her cheeks and jaw. Hands stroked her breasts lazily before dropping to caress her thighs. Her brain wasn't working very well, but all the other parts of her body were in tip-top shape. It didn't matter that some of the bits and pieces hadn't seen a lot of use lately.

They all had worked just fine, thank you.

James pressed his lips against her temple. "How're you doing, Kaylee Kat?"

He expected her to be able to speak? "Huh."

A long low chuckle escaped as James stroked his finger along the side of her neck. Tracing downward until his hand rested on the swell of her breast. "Me too," he agreed.

"If we have to be stuck in an elevator, I guess it's not so bad."

His laughter increased. "Are you saying you're suitably entertained?"

"Well," she began thoughtfully. "It's not quite as entertaining as the Marvel marathon you promised, but it'll do in a pinch."

A small shriek escaped as he literally pinched her butt and murmured a teasing warning. "Behave."

"Where's the fun in that?" Kaylee pressed her palms to his cheeks, examining his face carefully. "Are you okay? I don't know what to expect with the fever and all."

He shrugged. "I'm not too sure myself, but we'll be okay. Now that you've stopped avoiding the inevitable."

She'd stopped fighting him, but the worries remained. Temporarily boxed up because everything inside her still screamed it wasn't fair for James to be stuck with her.

But timing was everything. Once the truth became clear, they'd have to deal, but right now she was going to do everything she could to make sure he didn't suffer, to make sure he knew exactly how much she cared about him. It was the only thing she could think of to help ease the coming trouble.

Kaylee stroked her knuckles over the rough bristles on his cheek. "If there's anything else you need, let me know."

He cocked a brow. "Even though we're still trapped in an elevator?"

She sighed. "Like you said, we could be here for a while. I don't want you to suffer."

"Me neither. I think we should go find a hot shower and a soft bed for the next round."

It wasn't very ladylike, but she couldn't stop from snorting. "Sure. Let's get right on that."

A second later she was in the air again—*damn bear*—before being settled on her feet. She reached into space to catch her balance, but James was there, holding her tight until she was steady.

"Wait here," he ordered, sliding her hand to the solid metal of the elevator.

She leaned against the wall.

He scooped down and rummaged around in the backpack for a moment before moving to the elevator doors. He slid an oversized screwdriver into the slim slot between them and applied pressure until the narrowest gap appeared. With sheer brute strength, he slid the doors apart, darkness looming on the far side.

Kaylee stepped tighter against the wall. "Do fail-safe double redundancies still work when you open the door and —*oh my God*, what are you doing?" she shrieked as James scooped her up in his arms.

The low light from the flashlights in the corners cast eerie shadows on his face as he grinned, carrying her toward the deathtrap of an opening. "Heading for a bed."

She screamed as he stepped off into nothing—

A second later he absorbed the shock of landing, and she opened her eyes to discover they were standing in a dimly lit hallway. Behind them, the elevator doors stood open, the floor level with James's waist.

Kaylee lifted a fist and smashed it on his chest. "You *bastard*. You scared me to death."

Only she was laughing, and so was he as he reached back into the elevator. He grabbed one of the flashlights and passed it to her. "I really wish the security cameras were working, because watching your face right then would've been priceless."

"You're lucky I didn't pee my pants," she muttered.

A loud burst of laughter escaped. "You're hysterical, Banks."

"I should be hysterical," she said, resting one arm around his neck and extending the other arm forward so the flashlight illuminated the hallway. He strode toward the emergency exit with her cradled in his arms. "This is all moving a little quickly, and you did just throw us out of an elevator. I thought we were about to plunge to our deaths."

A low growl escaped him, and Kaylee shivered.

Good grief, what *was* it about his growling? Or more to the point, what was it was doing to her libido? Sure, there was tons of lingering sexual tension between them, but the sound drove her way past anticipation as fiery heat slid over her skin.

She glanced at his face.

"Since we're going back to my apartment to continue to enjoy the mating fever, I hardly think I'd do anything stupid to mess that up. I want you, Kaylee, and now there's nothing to stop us."

Not even, it seemed, nine flights of stairs.

"I. Can. Walk," Kaylee said between bounces as he rushed upward.

He ignored her, running with her in his arms at a pace that far outstripped anything she would've been able to do. So...win?

They reached the top floor, and he shouldered opened the door to his suite without letting her go. There were signs everywhere of her rapid escape, including soggy jeans abandoned on the floor.

James stepped over them and headed straight for the back of the apartment. When he stepped into the bathroom, she laughed.

"I feel as if we've done this before," Kaylee teased. "Maybe even earlier today?"

He put her down. "I hate to admit my memory is a little foggy."

Oh. "The mating fever."

He turned on the shower and steam began to rise. "It's

71

funny. I can tell it's there, but it's not muddling my brain like it did earlier."

"Your bear was pretty hard in charge," she told him. "And while I like that side of you..." *Oh dear.* There wasn't really any polite way to say this. "You're not always the sharpest tool in the shed when you're in that form."

He was stripping away her clothes, and his, then bringing her into the shower with him. "It's not an insult. I don't think many polar bears get smarter in their animal form. Better at scenting, yes. And fighting, if it involves brute strength. I think most shifters are smarter in their human forms."

I'd disagree with that, her cat commented even as she purred smugly, gloating at the heated contact between James's naked body and Kaylee's.

Be quiet, Kaylee scolded.

Then all conversation, internal and otherwise, was over. James had something on his agenda other than talking, and in a matter of moments, Kaylee was breathing way too hard to be able to speak.

He touched her delicately. Reverently. As if she were a precious gift he hadn't expected to receive.

As the heat flared in his eyes, his touch became more possessive. His fingers gripped a bit harder, his caress got a little needier.

James loomed over her, her shoulders pressed hard to the tile. He had one arm over her head, his gaze fixed on hers.

"We've never done this before," he reminded her right before sliding his hand down to cup her sex possessively.

The squeak that escaped was embarrassing, but a little less so than the moan that followed hard on its heels as he slipped his fingers between her folds. She was wet—and it had nothing to do with the shower.

His smile was beyond cocky.

"You smell delicious," he informed her.

Her response was stolen away on a gasp as his thumb pressed hard against her clit and he slipped two fingers into her core.

Kaylee wrapped her fingers around his forearm, not to keep him away but because—

Oh my God, she didn't know *why*. She needed to hold on to something or she was going to melt away and disappear down the drain.

"So wet. So slick and tight." James hummed happily as he pulled his fingers back then plunged in again.

She really had no say in the matter because telling him she didn't want this would be a lie, and it was obvious stopping was the last thing on his agenda. The look of delight in his eyes as his gaze remained fixed on hers was as amazing as the pressure building in her core.

"*James,*" she whispered, her legs trembling so hard only the fingers inside her were keeping her upright.

"It's okay," he assured her. "I've got you. I need this."

That made two of them. Under her fingers, the muscles of his forearm continued to flex. Bands of steel rotating like a mechanical fucking device made specifically for her pleasure.

He sped up, fingers going deep and finding the perfect spot inside her to send her shooting off into space. Her core clutched his fingers, while the sounds and scent of sex rose into the steam around them.

Her legs were still shaking when he dropped to his knees, and suddenly it was his tongue on her, teasing her clit as his fingers continued to torment her, and what she

VIVIAN AREND

thought was an end became the start of a whole new orgasm. Faced with too much pleasure to keep still, her thighs rattled against the wall behind her.

James pressed a hand across her belly to hold her upright, but he didn't stop and neither did her orgasm.

He ended up catching her as she slipped toward the ground, swinging her into his lap in a repeat of the position they'd been in earlier that day. Only now, they were both naked, and the thick length of his erection pressed against her clit.

A hard pulse struck inside her core. A continuation of her earlier orgasm? Kaylee didn't think she'd stopped, but as mindless as she felt, she knew what she wanted right now.

There was little doubt that he'd enjoy it too.

No need for a condom—with no sexual diseases amongst shifters, and her birth control, there was nothing to do but rise up on her knees and reach between her legs to catch hold of his thick length.

James swore and then his fingers were on her chin, lifting her gaze to meet his. "*Kaylee.*"

She angled him backward, rocking her hips to cover the tip with her slickness. "I'm very glad you didn't do something stupid like tell me it would be okay to wait."

"You hate it when I lie," he said bluntly.

Then he was roaring because she was sliding over him, his cock pressing into her sex. Filling her to the brim and setting off another round of explosions.

She'd been staring at him as she moved. His eyes squeezed shut and his face contorted into the most pained expression she'd ever seen. "You okay?"

Hot water beat down on them, and steam filled her lungs with every breath, but as he opened his eyes, it was all

James. He was the cause of the heat rolling over her body. Igniting her senses and sending pleasure soaring.

He wrapped his arms around her, taking hold of the back of her neck. "Never been better," he assured her. "Never."

He kissed her, tangling their tongues, stroking into her mouth as he stroked into her body. The arm around her tightened, and he lifted her enough so he could move back then plunge deep. Intimate connection, bodies sliding together. He filled her senses.

He filled her.

Not just physically—although, *whoa, nelly on that one*— but he was touching her in a way that said he cared. As he kissed his way along her jaw and nibbled on her ear, he murmured soft words that said he knew exactly who he was with. That he wanted to be there.

"You're mine," James growled softly. "Right now, and tomorrow, and the day after tomorrow. I choose you."

To hell with it. When a guy was that damn sweet, it was time to admit defeat. "Okay."

He chuckled. "Okay?"

She fought to keep from giggling, at least until he thrust up so hard the laugh became a moan, and then she was coming again. Different, better, because she was squeezing around his cock, and his eyes were rolling back in his head, and he was making noises as if he had just won the lottery.

And as they clung to each other afterward, she had to admit it was a pretty powerful thing to be able to see James Borealis lose it.

Now she had to find the strength to make sure he never regretted it.

10

So much for going slow.

They weren't even dried off before James dropped her on the bed. He joined her before she finished bouncing so he could ravish her all over again.

He was a gentleman, though. Mostly. He made sure he licked every inch of her body thoroughly until she was gasping before covering her and pressing his cock deep.

The third time they finished screaming in pleasure, collapsing onto the mattress like boneless cuts of meat, Kaylee flapped a hand at him and moaned. "Time out. Oh my God, *please*. I call timeout."

James took a deep breath and considered. "I might be able to stop for a while."

Something that sounded suspiciously like *goddamn sex fiend* escaped her lips.

He rolled, intending to curl himself around her. When his hand accidentally slipped up to cup her breast, she caught hold of his pinkie and twisted it hard until his hand slid downward. "Timeout means if you touch any of my erogenous zones in the next fifteen minutes, I'll cut you into small pieces."

"What if I accidentally—?"

To his amusement, a vicious growl escaped her.

James nuzzled against her neck. He kept his hand safely pressed against her belly because, well, while he wasn't allowed to fondle any of the good bits, *all* of her felt stroke-worthy.

It took a long time for their heart rates to return to something near-normal. And while more sex was definitely on the agenda, when their stomachs both rumbled simultaneously, James had to admit it. "I finally need food more than I need fucking."

"Thank God. Not that the fucking wasn't spectacular, but I'm starving," Kaylee warned him.

She slipped out of his arms and into the shower, and this time he let her be alone.

Food, his stomach reminded him. They could have another go at shower sex later.

Not too much later, though.

James checked his messages while Kaylee had a quick rinse, but there really wasn't anything dire on his to-do list work-wise for the next week. Now that Cooper knew what was going on, James was sure the rest of his family would be warned he was unavailable.

Making plenty of time for him and Kaylee to enjoy themselves. Plus, time to deal with the worry that kept creeping into the delectable woman's eyes.

He didn't think she was even aware she was doing it. Going from smiling one moment like a cat that had caught the canary, to gnawing on her bottom lip and staring into space with trepidation.

James let his gaze drift over her as she returned to the

room. Nope, plenty of time for all the important things, including convincing her she was the best thing that had ever happened to him.

Kaylee paused in the middle of drying her hair to stare back at him before smacking him playfully on the arm. "My God, that's so annoying. Are you going to grin like that all week?"

"How do you want me to grin?" he asked before ducking out of range.

She was still laughing as he marched over to his dresser and pulled out a T-shirt. He tossed it at her, watching with amusement as she slipped the oversized garment over her head without removing her towel first.

Her modesty was going to kill him. "Seriously? What's that nonsense?"

"Some of us are not exhibitionists." Kaylee gathered up her things and headed toward the laundry room. Probably thought she was going to get to wash and dry her clothes. Well, fine, she could, but it's not as if she was going to be wearing much of anything for the next week. Not if he had a say in the matter.

He pulled on a pair of sweatpants out of consideration, though, and also because having his junk rise and fall like a barometer in a storm wasn't that entertaining.

While he planned on spending most of the week in bed, they couldn't spend *all* week there. Certainly not unless he fed her at regular intervals.

Her quick glance as she exited the laundry room made him realize again how far they had to go in this new relationship. The tension in her shoulders hadn't released until she'd confirmed he was partially dressed.

They'd been friends forever. But *only* friends—and he

had to remember that, no matter how natural it felt to have stepped beyond that boundary.

But now, as he followed her into the kitchen, the need to protect was fierce. Not only to keep her safe from outside harms, but from everything inside that was making her unhappy.

As she pulled open the refrigerator door, he placed his hand over hers. He carefully guided her backward, closing the door and pulling her into his embrace. "You're doing it again," he said softly.

Kaylee twisted until she could rest her head against his chest. "Sorry. I'm just worried."

"Let's make a deal. You're allowed to worry as long as I'm allowed to take care of you."

Kaylee snickered. "In other words, you think you get to boss me around."

"Only as much is I've ever been able to, Banks. Which is not at all."

He tucked his fingers under her chin and lifted until he could press a kiss to her lips. Slow and intense, but brief. He gave her a tight squeeze then backed away.

"Time to grab some food. Because while I seem to be having extraordinary control for someone in the midst of a mating fever, there's no guarantee it's going to last." Blunt speaking, but she'd better be prepared. "I won't do anything to hurt you," he said.

"Good grief, course you won't. Mostly because I would take you out at the knees if you tried," Kaylee informed him primly. "I know you, Borealis. We know each other. It's not the one-on-one time that I'm worried about."

It should be. If she had any idea of how much he was looking forward to taking her again...

They cobbled together a meal, but when she would

have put their plates on the table, he shook his head. He settled in his oversized easy chair and patted his thighs.

Kaylee raised a brow even as she made her way over to climb daintily into his lap. "What would you have done if I'd made soup instead of sandwiches?"

"Eaten very, very carefully," he assured her.

He'd begun to figure out that odd sensation tormenting his skin was only there when he didn't have a hand on her. "I'm going to be pretty touchy-feely for the next while," he warned.

"I have no problem with that." Kaylee, who had been his companion in mischief-making for far too many years to count, offered him a blinding grin. "I'm kind of living in a lust-filled haze right now. You being touchy-feely is not an issue."

Kaylee took a bite of her sandwich, lifting a finger to catch a dollop of mustard that had escaped and clung to the corner of her mouth. He couldn't take his eyes off her fingers as she licked them clean.

Her lips—mesmerizing.

They sat quietly for a while, fixated on the food. For good reason, since they must've burnt off a million calories in the past two hours.

Only when her plate was half empty did Kaylee let out a sigh and slow down.

"Is something supposed to happen?" she asked. "I mean, in terms of weird things going on."

"Maybe? I don't know for sure," he admitted.

Kaylee growled softly before taking a ferocious bite out of her sandwich. "I have to say this whole cone of silence is pretty stupid when it comes right down to it. You'd think male polar bear shifters would be more willing to share details."

"The only details I know guys dish about are ways to avoid getting trapped by the mating fever." He regretted the words as soon as they were out of his mouth because she looked sad again. "Kaylee, I didn't want to avoid the mating fever this year." Normally he never would've shared this intel, but considering they were going to be together forever, she needed to know.

"Grandpa gave us an ultimatum earlier this year. Says he wants the three of us mated or he'll sell Borealis to Midnight Inc. My brothers and I agreed we'd—" He stopped as the expression on her face changed from annoyance to concern to utter horror. "What?"

She sat stick straight and rigid in his arms. "Normally you would've done everything you could to avoid the mating fever. Grandpa Giles *forced* you to get stuck with me?"

Dammit, this was not going to end well.

"No, it wasn't like that," James began before he had to kind of acknowledge the truth. "Well, okay, it *was* like that, but he didn't force me. Really."

"I'm going to kill him." The fury in her eyes said she might not be joking.

"Hey, it's okay. I mean, yes, he was a bit of a jerk to lay down the law like that, but at the same time I'm glad."

Kaylee wouldn't meet his gaze. "Yeah, right, because you were just dying to end up trapped with me for the rest of your life."

Okay, enough of that bullshit. James caught her by the chin and turned her face toward his. Glaring, he let her see every bit of his annoyance. "You do that again and I'll put you over my knee. How many times do I have to tell you *I chose this*? Yeah, maybe my hand was pushed at the start, but this isn't a disaster, and *you're* not a mistake. And if you keep saying that, I'm going to get pissed off. Stop it, Banks. You're bloody perfect, and that's the end of the fucking story."

He glared at her. She frowned back.

The corner of her mouth twitched. Her entire body was one tight bundle, and she looked as if she were about to burst into tears.

Guilt sauntered in. "Oh, sweetie, I'm sorry I shouted at you."

Her lips quivered. Then again, harder, and he was about to apologize again when a burst of laughter hit him smack-dab in the face.

Memories flooded in of first seeing that same delight and amusement. Ten years old and thick as thieves since the moment her family had moved in next door to his. They'd become best friends overnight. Inseparable, whether playing, or fighting, or just dealing with growing up.

There was always laughter.

Like the time he'd decided he was going to shave. Which wouldn't have been a terrible disaster, except Kaylee, his ever-present friend, somehow convinced him that shaving included armpits, arms and legs as well as the peach fuzz growing on other parts of his body.

Hey, they saw that in commercials all the time, right? Yet it wasn't the shaving that had made her lose control and laugh like a hyena, but his screams after he'd realized the soap he'd lathered up with had been studded with cinnamon.

The memory blurred with others: years of homework, and camping in the backyard, and yard chores, and Halloweens spent together. The connection between them grew clearer in his mind than ever before.

James put their plates aside for safety's sake, ignoring

her laughter, which had devolved into giggles, slowly fading into hiccupping snorts.

He waited. A long time.

Her lips were still quivering as she placed a hand on his face. "You really need to learn how to speak your mind."

A wry smile escaped.

"I mean, how am I ever going to know what you're thinking when you won't share what you're feeling with me?" she teased.

She leaned in and kissed him, right on the tip of his nose.

He shook his head. "Nice try, baby, but that's not good enough."

Kaylee sighed as if hard done by. "You've said it clearly, so I will listen instead of arguing—"

"Can I get that in writing?"

"—and I believe you. You wanted this. And while I don't understand exactly why, I'm glad. Because you *are* my best friend. I want to make you happy."

James tapped his lips. "Then kiss me."

One of her brows rose. She leaned in and skimmed past his mouth to press her lips to his cheek.

"*Kaylee...*" he warned.

"Target practice," she insisted before covering his face with dozens of kisses. Moving along his jaw to his ear where she fucked up his mind completely by nibbling on his earlobe.

When she began working her way down his neck, James decided they'd definitely had enough to eat. It was time for La-Z-Boy sex.

---

11

*B*y the third day, Kaylee had learned things she'd never thought possible. Such as:

1) Polar bear shifters could climax and then continue fucking less than thirty seconds later.

2) Bears in a mating fever fucked more than they slept.

3) Her best friend was a wizard with his tongue.

Okay, that one she might've guessed was possible, but finding out for sure? Pure heaven.

For kicks, she hopped on the scale during a brief moment between being ravished in the shower and being ravished up against the wall of the hallway. She stared at the numbers in shock.

"What?" James asked, running his fingers down her side. He was rarely more than an arm's length away, which was fine by her because anytime he *was* farther than that she got this weird tugging sensation in her belly.

"I've lost ten pounds," she told him.

"I fed you," he insisted.

"I know you did," she said with a touch of exasperation. "It's all the weird bear tricks."

"I'll feed you more," he offered. "I was going to get groceries delivered this afternoon. Chinese takeout? Thai? Pizza? Actually, I'll just order all three. That'll make things easier."

"I want a meat lover's pizza with barbecue instead of red—" Kaylee began only to have James wave a hand and finish her sentence.

"—no red sauce. Extra cheese, and you want a side of chipotle dip."

They grinned at each other.

Her phone went off. Amber's ringtone.

Kaylee glanced at James, not because she was asking for permission but because they were in the middle of something pretty intense and she wanted to respect that.

His expression softened, and he stepped in, caressing a hand over her cheek. "I bet Amber's worried. I should've made sure you called her back right away."

"She knew you'd take care of me," Kaylee said firmly before grabbing her phone off the table.

"While you talk, I'll bring home the bacon." He offered her a heated leer. "You can reward me suitably later."

Kaylee gagged at him, amused as he crossed his eyes in retaliation.

She answered her phone before Amber could give up. "Hey. Everything's great."

Maybe if she kept telling herself that it would be true.

Her friend's voice played delicately in her ear. "Truly?"

The temptation to giggle was strong. "If you're asking for details, I'm not sure—"

"No. That's fine," Amber hurried to dissuade her. "I didn't expect *this*, though."

"That makes two of us," Kaylee admitted.

She'd planned on walking out onto the balcony, but

every step she took was as if an elastic between her and James grew thin and taut. Uncomfortable.

Instead of fighting the urge, she returned to settle on the arm of his chair. With a hand resting on his shoulder, she rubbed the back of his neck as he spoke quietly into his phone, a half dozen takeout menus scattered on the table in front of him.

"Is there anything you need?" Amber asked. "I've had a devil of a time trying to get any kind of information out of the boys. All they keep telling me is to not disturb you. I'm sorry, but I had to make sure."

"It's fine," Kaylee insisted. Her fingers drifted into James's hair. She played with it, tangling it in circles to enjoy the soft caress gliding against her palms. "He's got the fever, and I have to admit, it's been a lot of fun. And that's all I'm going to say about *that*."

An embarrassed chuckle carried over the line. Sweet Amber was such an innocent. They'd become good friends over the past couple years, and while free-love wild nights weren't a part of either of their lifestyles, as a shifter, Kaylee was used to blunter discussions about sex than the human.

"Do you feel different?" Amber asked.

Avoiding any kind of comment about sexual wear and tear, Kaylee thought it over. Her inner cat was pretty much snoozing contentedly, happy to be warm and dry. Other than that? "Nothing. But the week's not up yet. James doesn't seem to know much about how this works, either."

"I'll do some research. I mean more. I didn't want to dig too deep in case that was stepping over lines, but if you're interested..." Amber left the option open.

It wasn't going to hurt anything. "Go for it. Not much we can do at this point, anyway."

Kaylee jammed her lips shut against making some other

comment about how terrible she was going to be for James as a mate. She'd promised to try, and she was going to keep her word.

The thought of being by his side on a public stage, though, was enough to make her lose her appetite.

James was still ordering, but now he turned his attention on her and even while he was reading off an impossibly long list of items to the Thai restaurant, he slid his hand over her hip and under her shirt to rest his big warm palm against her lower back.

"That meeting we talked about." Amber spoke softly as if worried James would overhear. Or maybe there was someone in the office she was trying to avoid. "Next week. I assume you're going to be done with your... Done by then."

James's gaze drifted over her body. He slid his hand higher then scratched his nails gently down her spine.

Kaylee's body lit up with desire, but she focused on answering coherently. "I think so. Go ahead and set it up."

Her other line buzzed, and she was tempted to curse. "Gotta run. Love ya. Chat soon."

She hung up and switched to answer the other call.

"Mister Borealis," she said primly.

One of James's brows rose. Then damn if he didn't grin evilly and slide his hand around her torso until he cupped her naked breast.

"You know better, young lady," Grandpa Giles scolded her.

She wasn't ready to forgive the man. Not considering everything that was still up in the air. "Was there something you needed, sir?"

In front of her, James clicked his tongue in warning even as his smile widened with mischief. "He's not going to like that," he murmured.

"I don't care—" Kaylee sucked in a sharp breath because James had shoved up the edge of the T-shirt and was now teasing his tongue over her nipple.

"Just wanted to say thank you for getting those papers signed. Contract went off without a hitch because of you. Damn smart woman."

Kaylee's brain was rapidly turning to mush as James upped his game. Nibbling now before closing his lips and pulsing softly.

She fought for some sort of response, made easier because James's grandfather was laying on the BS way too thick. "It was nothing, sir. Only took a moment of my time, and then the rest of the evening was mine."

Oh my God, it felt so good. She jammed the free hand that wasn't holding the phone into James's hair, trying to drag him to the other side because only half her body was pulsing, and that really wasn't fair.

It took a moment for her to realize that on the other end of the line, Grandpa Giles had gone silent. "Only took a moment. Well, that's good. Glad there wasn't any trouble. Sometimes that James needs a little extra help."

James seemed to be multitasking just fine at the moment. He'd shoved the shirt up over both her breasts, cupping them together so he could more easily switch from one side to the next.

Kaylee slid until she was straddling his thigh, needing pressure on other parts of her body.

"Oh, James was fine. Very independent. Or at least it seems that way to me. He and I always end up arguing about the stupidest things." Like how he shouldn't be messing with her while she was trying to have a grown-up conversation.

"But he wasn't feeling well. Summer fever... Or something."

Oh, really? It was almost as if he'd known James might be teetering on the edge of mating fever. And now the old goat was fishing for information.

Tough luck. Kaylee not only didn't feel like informing him of any details, she was rapidly losing all interest in the entire conversation. "James? Feverish? Definitely not. When I left his apartment Friday, he was in tip-top shape and just as annoying as usual."

"Ahhh." Grandpa Giles seemed confused.

Okay, it was a lie, but it was none of his business and he deserved to suffer a little.

"Sorry, need to run. Glad your meeting turned out well, Mr. Borealis."

She hung up, tossing her phone onto the couch so she could reach down and haul James's lips up to hers.

He kissed her for a moment, his smile clear as their mouths connected. He pulled back just far enough to keep dragging his fingernails gently down her back, rocking her over his thigh in an intimate, sensual tease. "Poor Grandpa Giles. He's probably freaking out right now, trying to figure out what the hell's going on."

"Poor Grandpa Giles, my ass. The man deserves to suffer a little," Kaylee said bluntly. "Did you order enough food to feed an army?"

"I did."

She slid a hand between them and wrapped her fingers around the thick length of his cock pressed against his thin sweatpants. "How long do we have before the supplies arrive?"

"An hour," he told her proudly. "Which gives me plenty of time to ravish you."

She attempted to look as if she were seriously considering his comment as he rose to his feet and carried her toward the bedroom. "I suppose that's enough time for a modest ravishing. We'll have to save the thorough ravishing for later."

"A brilliant plan."

The modest ravishing was followed by massive amounts of food, and then a thorough ravishing.

The next day's schedule was pretty much the same, although when Grandpa Giles tried phoning James, he didn't bother to answer.

By the time they lay in bed six days after the storm had rolled through, Kaylee felt well used and very, very content.

James lay next to her in the bed, stroking his fingers over her belly. He pushed up on one elbow and watched his hand as he caressed. "I think we've reached the beginning of the end," he warned. "I mean, I still want to do terribly dirty things to you, but it's no longer a dire need... Well, that's not right. The compulsion to get down and dirty with you is just as strong, but it's..."

He made a face, and she laughed. She knew what he was trying to say.

James rolled her on top, draping her sated limbs over his rock-solid chest. "Fuck it. This is coming out all wrong because there's nothing that's changed in terms of how much I want you. But I *can* tell the fever's abating."

She sighed. "It's been lovely. I suppose at some point we have to get back to reality."

His grin said he agreed. Then his expression softened, and he took a deep breath. "So. Do you feel...different?"

Kaylee opened her mouth and prepared to rip out her heart.

12

Kaylee had been thinking hard about this very thing. While she hadn't had very much time to go online, considering how busy James had kept her, Amber had forwarded her a bunch of links. Kaylee had stolen moments to pore over the data in the hopes she could figure out what she should be looking for, trying to figure out exactly what mating was supposed to feel like in the *my God, this is really happening* stages.

None of it seemed applicable. "I don't think so. I mean, I feel like I know you better—and no making a smartass comment about that—than I did a week ago. I feel closer to you. But in terms of any mystical magical woo-woo... Nothing."

"It's okay. It might take time to kick in." He sounded so confident, the same way he had when they'd been trapped —*ha!*—in the elevator.

No. Wait...

He sounded even cockier than that. Something was up. "Why? Do *you* feel different?"

"Oh, no. No, no, no, no. Nothing yet." Then of all

things, he started to straighten the sheets around them. Fussing for no reason.

Oh. My. God. Kaylee pushed up to a sitting position and stared at him. "You do. You do feel something."

"It's okay if we don't talk about it right now," James began before she raced to cut him off.

"Please don't," Kaylee begged. "I can't tell if you're teasing, or if you're trying to not disappoint me, but I can't take it."

A rumble escaped him that sounded as if he were ready to go into battle. James scooped her into his lap. He rubbed a hand over her back as she hid her face against his chest. His voice went lower, his arms a protective shield around her. "I'm not teasing, but I don't want you to feel pressure. Mating takes both of us accepting our fate, and I don't want you to feel as if you were forced into being with me."

Great. So, she had a shot at forever with the one man who'd always had a piece of her heart, and yet now, when she had just begun to hope, something was so screwed up inside her that she was going to miss out on being with him. "I don't feel forced. I *want* to be with you," Kaylee insisted. "You're my best friend."

James nodded slowly. "Which is why we should give it a little more time."

"But you feel something?" she whispered, frightened for him to straight-up answer. Frightened that he wouldn't.

His lips pressed to her temple. "Yes. I feel something. Right here."

He grabbed her hand and pressed it against his chest. Under her fingers his heart beat, strong and sure.

"I don't know how to describe it other than *potential.* Like a seed that's been planted but needs more sunlight to grow. Or a treasure chest that will open as soon as we turn the key, and everything I've ever needed will be inside."

His words were poetic and beautiful and made something inside her long even harder. "Then I should have the key."

Kaylee closed her eyes and tried everything she could barring rubbing her hands over her own body. She was sore in all sorts of lovely places, and she had no idea what she was looking for.

Not true. She knew exactly what she was looking for—a future with her best friend. No matter that she was probably going to muck things up for him at some point, she was selfish enough to want what she wanted.

She wanted him with all her heart.

Didn't she?

James lifted her chin and stared into her eyes before opening his mouth. He was about to do something big and heroic, and she didn't think she could handle it.

Distraction, now. "We need to count our silver linings. I mean, you lived up to your part of your bargain and didn't try to avoid the fever. So your brothers and grandpa have to be satisfied, no matter what happens between us."

She turned toward him and had to forcibly untangle their legs, because the thought of moving away seemed wrong—it wasn't a magical, mystical connection, but a really deep longing lodged in her gut.

"I *want* you to be my mate," James said.

"I know."

But the truth was *they* weren't in control. Fate was.

Kaylee pushed aside her fears. Obviously, fate knew better than James did who would be good for him going forward, and if she wasn't it, she would force herself to be happy for him.

"This isn't over," he growled, frustration in his eyes as his fingers clung to hers. "We aren't done."

"What if we're not mates—"

James twirled them and had her pinned to the mattress in a matter of seconds. Both he and his bear stared down. "Answer truthfully. Do you want to be with me, Kaylee Banks? As more than a friend, as more than my lover. Do you want me forever?" he demanded.

"Yes." The answer came instantly. It wasn't something she had to think about.

His lips curled. "Then there isn't anything we need to worry about. Maybe the mating instinct will kick in sometime during the next few days. Heck, maybe it'll take a little longer for it to arrive. But it doesn't matter, because I *choose* you, got it?"

She tipped her head, astonished that he just kept giving and giving. Shame snuck in. "I'm sorry."

James brushed a strand of hair off her forehead, tucking it behind her ear. "It's not your fault that the mating sign hasn't shown up."

"It's not that. I've just been so stupid this past week. I mean, between moments of absolute brilliance, of course."

She succeeded in pulling a laugh from his lips. "Tell me one of your brilliant moments," he teased.

"Getting into bed with you. Fooling around in the shower. And on the hall side table. And on top of the dryer."

"The dryer was especially brilliant," he agreed. He kissed her softly. "Then what are you saying sorry for?"

"For not grabbing hold of the amazing truth you've been telling me ever since I showed up here that first night, soaking wet." She cupped his face in her hands and stared into his eyes. "You've told me a dozen ways that you want me. I'm not used to hearing it, but that's going to change.

I'm going to change. Down the road there are still things I'm not going to be able to do, and we're going to have to figure out workarounds, because I don't want to cause you any trouble or your family—"

"Except for Grandpa Giles. We can cause him trouble."

She rubbed her thumb along his cheekbones. "Definitely trouble for Grandpa Giles, but everything else we'll figure out together. That's what I'm saying sorry for. For not catching on to that sooner."

The kiss he gave her was sweet and tender. "Apology accepted, Banks. Now, I feel as if I've had a sudden relapse. I just can't hold myself back any longer."

Kaylee squealed as James dropped between her thighs. An instant later he had her stripped, his mouth over her sex, and was eating greedily. She clutched the comforter with both hands, fighting for control, but there wasn't much of a chance considering who she was dealing with.

One determined bear who wasn't going to give up on them.

She closed her eyes, and for the rest of the night, pleasure overwhelmed her.

James grinned at her over the breakfast table the next morning. "I need to go into the office to do some planning for the Canada Day celebration. I should be able to get off early this afternoon to help you grab your stuff."

Kaylee paused. "What am I grabbing to go where?"

He picked up their dirty plates off the table and stacked them in the sink. "Funny one, Banks."

"No, I'm serious," she insisted.

"We need to get your stuff so you can move in with me. I mean, you don't need to bring everything. Definitely not too many clothes. Forget all pyjamas as you're never going to need them ever again, but the rest of your stuff—"

Kaylee took a deep breath and mentally did a check. She'd promised to seize the future with him with two hands, and while her initial reaction was *this is going way too fast*, was it really?

Sort of. But she could work with that.

"What I'll do is pack a bag with the things I need for the next while, but I'm keeping my apartment. Not because I plan to run away again, but just because."

James shrugged. "You're paid up to the end of the month, so I suppose there's no real rush. You probably have to give a month's notice, so if we plan on doing the big stuff at the end of the summer, does that give you time to wrap your brain around this?"

The tension eased out of her. "Thank you for understanding. That sounds really good."

"I can give you a ride to your place later," he offered.

Kaylee shook her head. "I need to head there this morning to pick up my cameras for the shoot this afternoon, and I'm meeting Amber when she's done with work today. Just for drinks."

He snorted. "I bet she's got a million questions. She's going to talk your ear off, but I can hardly blame her. Chances are my brothers will do the same when I touch base with them."

She wasn't going to pretend. "It seems a little weird for us to be doing what we're doing, considering there's nothing official between us. The mating thingamajig, I mean."

"Then it's weird. So what?" He tapped her on the nose. "Do me a favour and drop my clothes off at work? I need to stretch and run for a while before I head in. I haven't been very nice to my bear, keeping him locked away this entire week."

She grinned. "Our animal sides knew we were more interested in being human to deal with all that 'sex stuff.'"

He echoed her grin. "Damn right."

Kaylee stroked her hands over his chest, just because she could. "Now that we're a little more balanced, my cat looks forward to going for a run with you."

He caught her fingers and pressed a kiss to her knuckles. "Come with me now," he offered.

Kaylee shook her head. "I have that appointment I need to make, but soon."

"My bear likes running with you." A sharp nip at her knuckles as heat flashed in his eyes. "He likes your pussy too."

She snorted. "You're terrible."

He is terrible, but kind of cute, her cat agreed before vanishing once again.

Fifteen minutes later they were downstairs. Kaylee stood beside her truck as James stripped off his layers. So reminiscent of a week earlier, but so much had changed.

He waggled his brows as he folded his pants then stacked them with the rest of the clothes in her outstretched arms. "Quickie?"

Kaylee laid the clothes on top of the hood of the truck. "Is that really what you want me to be talking about with my girlfriend? How fast off the mark you are?"

He was still laughing as he kissed her. His lips hardened, and his grasp grew possessive, and she was left breathless when he pulled away and shifted. The swirl of lights and heat were close enough they brushed her skin, and she felt as if she'd been kissed everywhere they touched.

Then the massive bear that was James paced around

her, heavy paws landing lightly on the concrete as he stroked his side against her like an overgrown kitten.

She reached out and tangled her fingers in his fur impulsively, petting as he rumbled in pleasure. He walked away with a lumbering grace, and she watched him go, part of her thinking it all had to be a dream.

13

*J*ames took the long route to get to work and didn't feel one bit guilty. He figured he was still off the clock until he stepped through the doors, and his wild side needed a little fresh air.

Didn't mind being cooped up so much, his bear informed him.

The bastard had a gloating tone in his voice, and James chuckled even as he responded as usual.

Shut up.

What? You had fun, I had fun. Just saying.

He'd never doubted that the wild side of him would be content with Kaylee around, but as they bashed through the trees and splashed through the creeks, he paused. He didn't want to assume, so he officially posed the question. "Do you know why Kaylee doesn't feel the mate connection yet?"

Nope. Maybe it's the cat thing. His other half was far more pragmatic. *You keep her, though. I like her.*

That made two of them.

As strange as it seemed, that bit of reassurance did a lot for the concerns that had been lingering in the back of his brain. James grabbed his clothes from where Kaylee had left them in his unlocked car.

Five minutes later, he was strolling through the back corridors of Borealis Gems, peeking in the windows and waving at familiar faces.

Everyone waved back, some smiles turning into outright smirks. Seemed news had travelled fast, and everyone knew why he'd been MIA for the last week.

He was just about to take the stairs up to Cooper's office when Grandpa Giles and Alex appeared, walking toward him.

"There you are."

James debated disappearing through the emergency exit, but he hadn't run from his grandpa since he was eight years old and had broken a window in the old man's study.

He shoved his hands in his pockets. "Here I am."

Grandpa bore down on him eagerly. Alex followed, walking at a slower pace. There was amusement in his eyes, but he shook his head slightly as if sympathetic for the coming storm.

"So?" Grandpa Giles demanded.

James met his gaze straight on. How exactly should he torment the old man?

Simple. Kaylee had given him the perfect idea.

"As requested, I fulfilled my part of the bargain and did not avoid the mating fever." He turned from his grandpa and spoke to Alex. "Can we meet about the security for the Canada Day event? I have a couple questions about the sound system and backstage access—"

He was interrupted by a small coughing fit. Probably Grandpa Giles choking on all the things he wanted to say but couldn't.

Alex somehow kept a straight face and patted the old

man on the back. "I'll be done with Gramps in about twenty minutes. We can meet then."

"Sounds great—"

"You didn't answer my question, boy." Grandpa Giles glared at him. "And I didn't demand anything. Just pointed out that responsible young men in most families would be happy to do their duty and—"

"—mate on command? Breed?" James offered helpfully.

This time, Alex had to cough to hide his amusement.

Grandpa Giles was still simmering. "Don't you get too big for your britches, young man," he said as he shook his finger in James's face.

"Believe me, I speak for myself, Alex, and Cooper when I tell you the last thing we want you worrying about are our britches. You've made your point. Now don't expect us to allow you to meddle any further in our lives." While Grandpa sputtered, James took the opportunity to offer a hidden wink to his brother. "See you in half an hour."

Then he pushed through the door at his back and headed up the stairs, already planning how he was going to share the recap with Kaylee for her amusement.

He found a pile of work stacked on his desk but managed to get through most of it before Alex joined him.

His brother placed a cup of coffee in front of each of them before settling in the comfy chair James had deliberately purchased for kicking back in. "Obviously you're feeling chipper."

"Feeling something," James agreed. He raised his cup and took a deep sip of the hot liquid, humming contentedly as it went down. He glanced across at Alex who was drinking quietly and eyeing him, a whole lot of questions visible in his expression.

"You're showing amazing restraint," James said drily.

"I'm torn between admiration and terror," Alex confessed. "So. Mating fever. And...*Kaylee?*"

Well, that was getting to the point. James spoke slowly. "Kaylee. Which is perfect, except for the fact that she's not feeling the mating connection yet and I am."

Alex's lazy laid-back attitude vanished. He perched at the front of his chair, staring at James in horror. "What? How? I mean, *why not?* She's been crazy about you for years."

James picked his jaw off the floor. "Get out. We've only been friends."

Alex rolled his eyes as only an older brother could. "Yeah. Friends who had the hots for each other. God, sometimes it would drive me crazy to be stuck in the same room with you guys. You were made for each other."

"Exactly what I thought. Which is why when Grandpa decided to pull his Machiavelli trick, I decided to move proactively. I always liked spending time with Kaylee. Now we've gone and had this week, and it was incredible and wonderful, and..." He took a deep breath before spitting it out. "At the risk of sounding like an idiot, what if she *doesn't* want me? She said she did, and she promised to do whatever it takes to trigger the mating bond, but obviously, something's missing."

His brother's expression grew more concentrated. "You set this up? You wanted to end up mated with Kaylee?"

"Of course. I figured with everything else we had going for us, we had a good shot."

"Interesting." Alex looked thoughtful. Then he shook his head and focused on James again. "You've got a couple choices. One, you wait. Maybe it takes a while for the connection to kick in on her end. You sure you feel it?"

James nodded. He laid a hand over his chest and that

hot swirl of possibility pounded hard enough it shook his very soul. "It's there, I swear it is."

"Maybe she's not aware of what it feels like at her end."

Also possible.

"Well, until she feels it, she can hardly accept it." Which was what made this all so frustrating. James waved a hand in the air. "Change of topic—give me the details for the Canada Day project. I may as well distract myself until Kaylee is free."

"Cooper wanted to get together," Alex told him as he adjusted position to reach the security diagrams scattered on the table. "He's been worried about you. We both were. Drinks after work?"

Perfect. If they happened to accidentally run into Kaylee as she met with her friends, the more the merrier.

"Don't worry about me," James said. "Whatever it takes to make this happen, I swear I'll get it done."

14

---

*K*aylee spent most of her morning doing menial tasks as reality snuck in far too quickly.

Between the mess of business emails she had to deal with and the private portraits she'd been hired to shoot, it was noon before she actually got to slow down long enough to let her brain catch up with everything else that had gone on.

It was a good thing the only work she'd had on the calendar during the past week had been for Borealis Gems, and all things considered, they'd probably understand why she'd rescheduled. Even though she'd only been gone a week, her apartment seemed colder and lonelier than ever.

Her email pinged, and she glanced over to discover a message from her parents.

Oh joy, oh bliss.

She debated deleting it unread, but because it had been six months since they'd last contacted her, *and* because she was a glutton for punishment, she clicked it open.

Hello, darling. I trust that all is well.

I deposited more money into the joint account in case you need it. Don't worry. We don't expect you to pay us back.

We have wonderful news. We've been asked to join a brand-new research project in the Romanian mountains. We'll be here for at least another six months.

Unfortunately, that means we won't be home next week, and I'd arranged delivery of a number of packages to the house. Some of it is delicate equipment that needs to be put into the shop immediately. I'll forward the message when I get word it's arrived.

Relying on you to make sure this gets taken care of.

Will update ASAP.
M&F

Kaylee let out an exasperated sigh. "Hi. Sure, everything is just peachy over here. I'm potentially going to end up mated to my best friend, if I can ever get my shit together enough to figure out what's wrong with me. But of course I want to hear about your world travels in spite of the fact that you can't bother to write me except when there's something you need. Oh, but I'm sure if you throw money at the situation, that will make everything better."

She stared at the computer screen, anger rising inside.

Inside, her cat snarled, furious and pissed off to the extreme, and that alone was enough to trigger action.

It took one deliberate click to send the email to print. Kaylee snatched the paper out of the tray the instant it was done so she could take it with her as she marched into the kitchen.

The entire time she rambled out loud as if having a reasonable conversation. "Of course, I won't have anything to do between now and then, so I'm happy to drop everything in order to deal with your delicate items that were probably broken in transit. And when you do eventually open them, you're going to blame anything that *is* broken on me."

She grabbed a pair of scissors and laid them on the counter.

Then she took the piece of paper and shook it hard. "And that's not to mention that the fact you won't be here means you're going to miss my birthday. *Again.*"

She took the paper and crumpled it into a tiny ball. Then she opened it up and crumpled it again.

She dropped the ball on the floor and stomped on it with her heels until the crinkled wad was a flat mess.

Then she opened it up, carefully folded it into a thin strip the best she could considering how crinkled the material was now. Strange how immensely satisfying it was to cut the mutilated origami into dozens of tiny strips.

She grabbed the mess, threw it in the sink, then put a lighter to it. The paper slowly caught fire, red crinkling along the edge before the entire bundle flashed upward.

As she stared at the flames burning in her kitchen sink, Kaylee straightened and let all of her annoyance pour out.

"You're *not* allowed to do this to me anymore," she said. "You're not allowed to make me feel inferior or worthless because what I expect and what you give are two separate things. I have had enough."

She folded her arms over her chest, feeling a little like a superhero as smoke billowed up from the paper.

"You know what? Those packages can sit on the damn porch and get rained on. Animals can come and sniff them and bite them and piss on them for all I care. I will no longer jump when you ask. Because *James* would never expect me to do something like that. If he wouldn't expect me to, then it's probably not on the *have to do* list."

A tremble started inside. A sense that she had just offered fate a challenge, and even though there was no way her parents could possibly know what she'd shouted, a shiver ran up her spine.

The fire alarm wailed.

Kaylee gasped in horror and reached for the faucet. Only, when she turned it on to try and put out the fire, the spray nozzle was pointed in the wrong direction and water hit her square in the face.

Suddenly, she was soaking wet.

She twisted the spray in the proper direction. Abandoning the nozzle in the sink, she climbed on a chair and reached up to open the fire alarm and remove the battery to stop it from breaking her eardrums.

Kaylee got the fire in the sink extinguished, then stood there, water dripping off the end of her nose as her ears rang, laughter bubbling up from deep inside.

Okay. That had been an exercise in how not to throw a hissy fit.

She washed the smoke smell out of her hair, packed a bag and threw it in the back of the truck. Then she headed across town to the Diamond Tavern, the bar that James owned with his brothers.

They'd opened for business about a year before taking on extra duties with the family gem business, and now it was one of the happening places in town. Bears did love to party, and so did the rest of the humans and shifters in the north.

The local wolves, the Orion pack, owned their own place to howl on the north edge of town. Sirius Trouble tended to draw an even wilder crew than Diamond saw most nights.

James had said he wanted something between a casual place to kick back and a destination for food and entertainment. With most of the clientele being shifters, everything was big, bright, and easy to replace.

Just because the Diamond had a less volatile caliber of guests than the Sirius, it didn't mean fights weren't an everyday occurrence.

Amber was already at the back bar, sitting with a woman whose silvery white hair was partially hidden under a black beanie.

Kaylee slid onto the bench seat next to her friend, accepting the hug she was offered gratefully. "I thought we'd have a few minutes alone," she whispered.

The beautiful woman across from them held out her hand. "Sorry about that. I got here early and didn't think sitting in the parking lot was a good idea. With my luck, someone would think I was casing the joint." The shifter winked then introduced herself. "I'm Lara. And remember, I have really good hearing. If you guys need to talk privately, I'll go to the washroom."

Kaylee eyed her, wondering what Lara was talking about.

One sniff later and the hackles rose on her inner cat—well, not literally, but still the truth was crystal clear. Lara was a wolf. While most shifters had better senses than the average human, wolf hearing was legendary.

Kaylee dipped her head. "Thanks for the warning, but

it's okay. I've had quite a week, but Amber and I can get caught up later. I'm looking forward to getting to know you."

"Me too. You guys..." Lara looked down into her glass and swirled her ice for a moment. "I don't have a lot of girlfriends to chat with. This is kind of special."

Under the table, Amber laid her hand on Kaylee's leg and gave it a tight squeeze.

Kaylee glanced down to find a small piece of folded paper in her hand. Awkwardly, Kaylee waited until Amber and Lara were discussing appetizer options so she could glance stealthily at the message.

It was a series of three short sentences.

Youngest in family.
Sister Alpha of Orion wolf pack.
Security department, Midnight Inc.

Which was pretty much what Kaylee had figured out on her own.

Lara not only worked there, but was part of the family who owned Midnight Inc., Borealis Gems's biggest competitor.

"You ladies decide what you want?" The question came from the waiter who stood beside their table. He wore a flirtatious grin as he openly admired them. At least until his gaze landed on Lara.

His eyes widened.

Lara lifted a brow but didn't say anything.

He opened and closed his mouth a few times, glancing over his shoulder as if looking for backup.

Amber cleared her throat to get his attention. She glared sternly. "You have a problem?"

It was entertaining to watch the guy, who had to be six foot two and outweighed Amber by at least one hundred pounds, straighten as if he'd been caught with his hand in the cookie jar.

He shook his head vigorously then took their order, stealing away rapidly as if he were worried Lara would jump up from the far side of the table and shake him.

Or worse, Amber.

Lara tugged her hat down a little further and slumped in her seat. "Sorry about this, guys. We should've picked somewhere a little more neutral to meet."

"There's no rule that says you're not allowed here," Amber said quickly.

Kaylee backed her up. "I agree. And honestly, I don't think you could've got us to meet you anywhere else, because Diamond serves the best chicken wings in town."

A soft smile curled across Lara's face, and she sat up a little straighter. "Thanks. I appreciate it. More than you know."

She picked up her drink and held it in the air before making eye contact with Kaylee and Amber in turn. "To making new friends."

Kaylee clinked their glasses together. "To not truly knowing what we're doing but moving forward anyway."

A soft laugh escaped from Lara, and she raised her glass again. "Yeah. There's a lot of that going on, as well."

The music was loud, and there was enough action on the dance floor that pretty soon it became clear no one was taking that much of an interest in the fact that Lara had entered untypical territory.

The three of them spoke quietly about the secret issue Kaylee had uncovered. Lara shared what she could but had to shake her head when asked specific questions about the rumoured takeover.

"I haven't been back in town for long enough to dig into details. After years in Toronto, coming back and resettling into the pack is taking some time, but I'll get there." Lara glanced between them. "I thought it would be good to meet you two and try to establish a link in case I need to act quickly."

"It was a good idea," Amber agreed before eyeing Lara closely. "I'm glad you're willing to talk with us, but I'm a little confused about why. Don't you want your family to be number one?"

A sad expression drifted over Lara's face. "You know how people say blood is thicker than water?"

The two of them nodded.

"You ever actually read that quote in its entirety?" Lara asked bluntly. "The real meaning is a doozy, and a good philosophy. I love my sister, as annoying as she is, but trust is more important than whose family I was born into. I don't blindly support *anyone* if they're wrong-minded. Which means if my sister is cheating, lying or otherwise screwing around with peoples' lives, I want to know so I can make it right."

Amber caught Lara's hand and squeezed her fingers. "I'm sorry."

"Me too. I'm not one hundred percent sure, though. Hopefully this is all a rumour and I find out all the whispers are completely legal and aboveboard."

"We'll help how we can, but we're also glad to get to know you. Outside of intrigue and that kind of thing,"

The woman smoothed her silver-white braid for a moment before firmly lifting her gaze to meet theirs. "That makes me happy. I meant it earlier—I'm looking forward to having new friends."

Impulsively, Kaylee reached across the table and squeezed Lara's hand. "If you ever need to talk, call."

"Me too," Amber insisted. "Although if it's about shifter stuff, I'm good with a search engine, and not much else."

"I don't know. You're pretty decent for a human," Kaylee teased.

Amber stuck out her tongue.

Lara was the one who brought up the unmentionable topic, turning to Kaylee with a smile. "So, did you end up mated with your bear?"

"How did you hear about that?" Kaylee asked.

Their new friend wrinkled her nose. "Small-town gossip is small-town gossip, and wolves are compulsively snoopy. Honestly, you're always going to have curiosity on high when it comes to mating fever. Polar bears are the only shifters to get it, and they're close-lipped about what goes on. Since wolves recognize our mates pretty much from the first moment, I'm fascinated by the differences in how things shake out for other shifters."

Amber laid a hand on Kaylee's arm. "You don't have to answer, but hey—at least Lara understands the mating part, which I, the human in the group, do not."

Kaylee fidgeted with her napkin. "I want to be with him, but so far I don't feel anything unusual. Cats don't have fated mates, and I haven't felt any sharp tug or anything. I don't know. What's a mating bond supposed to feel like?"

"Like that moment when you've been holding your breath for too long, and if you don't get your head above water and suck in fresh air you simply know you're going to die. Imagine that moment, ongoing and urgent. At least with an unfulfilled bond."

Lara took a casual sip of her drink while Amber and Kaylee stared in astonishment.

Their new friend shrugged. "So I've been told."

Okay, then. "I don't feel anything like that, but James says he wants to be with me, and I want to be with him. So, we're going to see what happens."

Amber squeezed her fingers on the table. "Again, as the lone human in the group, that doesn't sound too weird. Sounds like dating, and then moving in together like most humans do."

"No, it's weird," Lara and Kaylee said simultaneously, which set all three of them laughing.

"What's so funny?" A deep voice sounded from two feet to Kaylee's left.

They all glanced up to discover not only had James shown up, but Cooper and Alex both stood waiting as well. Looming over the table like massive, overprotective bears—

Yeah. Exactly what they were.

"Are you going to ask us to sit down?" James teased.

"Sure," Amber responded quickly, tucking herself against the wall.

Kaylee slid into the middle of the bench seat to make room for James to join her and Amber. She would tease him later for being totally oblivious to the dirty looks Alex was tossing Lara's way.

Oh, well. The guys owned the bar. If there were any damages, they'd have to pay for them.

15

*A*s he sat next to Kaylee and pulled her against him, James couldn't think of anywhere else he'd rather be.

Her thigh was tucked tight against his, hips together. He kept an arm draped around her body, and inside, his bear breathed a sigh of contentment.

She leaned closer. Amusement tinged her voice as she whispered, "I hope you brought bail money."

On the opposite side of the table, the third woman, the one with the incredible eyes—brown shot with flecks of gold —snorted before busying herself examining the dessert menu. Alex had been forced into the space next to her, as Cooper rested on the outside of the bench seat.

They'd made the place to be as comfortable as possible for shifters of all sizes, but it still looked like there was crowding going on.

"You guys going to survive over there?" James asked.

Alex looked downright uncomfortable, easing away from Cooper to try and give him some elbow room as their oldest brother picked up his drink that had been delivered the instant they sat down.

Only moving sideways tucked Alex closer to the stranger, and neither of them looked as if they were enjoying themselves.

The woman with the white-blonde hair offered James a gentle smile that made her face light up. "I'm fine. You don't need to move on my account."

Alex picked up his glass and drank steadily instead of answering.

James linked his fingers with Kaylee's and smiled at her. "You and Amber get caught up yet?"

In the corner, Amber leaned her head out. "Not yet, but a really good gossip session takes a few days."

"Depends on how much there is to tell," Kaylee said.

"Oh, girlfriend. I think there's plenty to tell." Amber offered James a wink. "You let me know if I can help coordinate anything."

Plates of wings arrived, and a moment later, the entire surface of the table was covered with food and all sorts of dipping sauces. For a moment, hands moved faster than mouths as everyone dug into their favourites.

Then curiosity got the best of James, and he turned to the newcomer. "Why do you look so familiar?"

His middle brother snorted. "How do you not know this?"

"Because I haven't lived here for years," the woman said dryly, wiping her fingers clean then offering her hand to James. "Lara Lazuli."

He kept a smile in place because that's part of what he did; stay cool and collected in the midst of unexpected situations. Now Alex's discomfort made sense. Holy smokes

—Lara was the youngest daughter of the family that operated Midnight Inc., their biggest competitor.

Which meant this was a great opportunity to put the thumbscrews on his brother, since Alex appeared bent out of shape way beyond proportion by the harmless, petite woman.

James shook Lara's hand firmly. "Consorting with the enemy. I like it. It adds a kind of pep to the day."

Kaylee's elbow dug into his side. "Stop that. She's not the enemy, she's our friend."

"Really," Alex said, his voice low and emotionless. "You all got to be besties in an awfully short period of time."

Amber leaned her elbows on the table and rested her chin in the palms of her hands. She looked adorable, like some freaking tree fairy. "Didn't we? It's because women are wonderful and marvelous creatures."

Lara copied the cutesy position, batting her lashes at Alex. "Sugar, and spice, and everything nice."

He choked for a moment. Cooper helpfully patted Alex firmly between the shoulder blades.

Seeing Alex so on edge because of the delicately featured woman sitting next to him was a hoot. James was happy for the entertainment, and having Kaylee next to him made everything else in him content.

Cooper and Amber began a running back-and-forth banter about the schedule for the upcoming Canada Day gala. Coordinating the event was supposed to be James's gig, but while he'd been out of commission for the past week, things seemed to have progressed nicely without him.

Kaylee tapped him on the shoulder before he could dive into the conversation. "I need to use the little bobcat's room."

He stepped aside to let her out, hiding a smirk as both

Cooper and Alex slid from their side of the bench to let Lara out as well.

He turned to Amber and gestured to the other women who were already heading away.

She shook her head. "Nah. I'm good."

"I thought women only travelled to the washroom in packs," he teased.

Amber raised her beer stein in the air, offering him an amused expression. "This human woman has an amazing bladder capacity far, far beyond that of the average shifter."

Both his brothers laughed as they resettled behind the table then grabbed their drinks.

Cooper raised his glass in a toast to the small dark-haired woman. "May you always have more than what you need."

Alex edged forward, speaking softly, but insistently. "Seriously, what is *she* doing here? Lara, I mean."

Amber wiggled her way closer, leaning in as if she was about to share some big secret. She lowered her voice and announced with great excitement, "Having drinks with me and Kaylee."

His brother leaned back, disgruntled. "Amber."

"Alex," she repeated in the same tone.

Both James and Cooper fought to keep from snickering. It was so much fun to see the little human take control of a situation where she should've felt intimidated. Alex was not giving an inch, and right now he was in one hundred percent overprotective, overbearing bear mode.

It was obvious, though, that Amber felt completely comfortable in making it clear this was a no fly zone.

"You need to step back and mind your own beeswax, buster. I know you're the grand pooh-bear of security at Borealis Gems, but you're not in charge of who Kaylee and I spend time with." She was on fire and her eyes glinted.

A low grumble escaped Alex. "Pooh-bah."

Amber frowned. "What?"

"It's Grand Pooh-bah—me, as the head of security, yada-yada. Not pooh-*bear*. That's a stuffed animal in a stor—"

"I *know* who Pooh Bear is." Amber spoke so dryly that James snickered, covering it up when his brother flashed him a dirty look. She continued. "When and *if* I ever have something important to tell you, I will. Until then, keep your furry butt out of my business."

Alex still looked annoyed, but he gave a brief nod and stopped trying to push her around. The tension that had slowly built faded.

Cooper eased away as Amber relaxed and picked up her drink.

James let his gaze drift over the bar. Between Alex knowing better than to pick a fight with someone he couldn't win against, and Cooper acting as backup for his personal assistant, *if* she needed it, which wasn't likely, there was nothing James needed to worry about.

Kaylee and Lara were coming back toward the booth, walking side by side and laughing as they wiggled their way through the crowd to where he waited.

Until someone stepped in front of them.

James didn't recognize the man, or his friends, and he didn't want to go off the deep end if blocking the women's path had been an accident. He was on his feet anyway because, dammit all, Kaylee was *his* and he planned to take care of her, no matter what.

Blood rushed to his brain as fury rose, and he was moving rapidly across the floor.

The road block wasn't an accident. Somebody was looking for trouble.

"You're a sweet thing," the man said, raising a hand as if he were going to stroke his knuckle down the side of Kaylee's cheek. "Far too sweet to be hanging out with this kind of trash."

Kaylee knocked his hand away before he could touch her, even as another man reached for Lara.

Someone in his path raised a fist. James countered it in self-defense.

And then like most nights in a northern town once the violence had hit the floor, it kind of rumbled out in a widening wave until it encompassed the entire gathering.

Fists swung, bodies crashed. Tables creaked, and glassware shattered. Through it all, James moved forward like the bear he was. He wasn't aware of making impact, he only knew he needed to get to Kaylee as quickly as possible.

Wading forward, bodies flew out of his way as if teleported. Or maybe those were his fists connecting with convenient body parts.

But when he got to the other side of the crowd, Kaylee was standing with her arms folded over her chest, glaring at the first man who had tried to touch her.

The one who was currently lying on the floor, moaning.

"Kaylee." James rushed forward.

That's when he noticed Lara had another man on his knees, his body twisted into a painful position. She had one of his arms shoved up behind his back, and the fingers of her free hand were tangled in his hair, his head pulled in a painful angle.

Lara wore a disturbingly sweet expression as she spoke softly to Kaylee. "Rude people in this bar."

"Unusual crowd," Kaylee offered with equal saccharine sweetness. "Must be a full moon or something."

Behind Lara, at the edge of his peripheral vision, Alex and Cooper had another two of the troublemakers in headlocks. James's gaze remained locked on the man on the floor attempting to crab crawl to safety.

Blood pounded at the back of James's eyeballs. "You tried to touch Kaylee," he said. "Prepare to die."

16

Kaylee had a slight ache in her entire body. It was all good and well that James wanted to be her mate, but this? Seriously?

As the big galoot waded forward, she stepped in front of him, smacking into his chest. James stopped instantly.

"*Prepare to die?* Who do you think you are, Inigo Montoya?"

Under her hand, James's chest continued to heave, pulsing with each heavy breath. His bloodshot eyes seemed unfocused, and she could swear his fangs were slightly out as he attempted to find the man she sensed inching toward safety behind her.

"He touched you," James growled, far more animal than man.

"He did not," Kaylee said.

It was true. Between her knocking his hand away and Lara acting like a freaking ninja warrior princess by taking down the guy bothering Kaylee *and* the next one in the lineup, she'd barely had time to get worried.

"Touched you." This time it came out a roar.

Okay. Now it was time to get worried. There was no reasoning with him when he was like this. He was leaving human thought behind and moving rapidly to fight or flight.

And right now, his bear didn't have a flight reflex.

It was the only thing Kaylee could think of to stop bloodshed from occurring—well, more than the bloody noses and blackened eyes already visible strewn on the floor between their table and where they now stood.

She fisted the front of his shirt with both hands and dragged herself up against him, using her body as a shield in an attempt to calm him down.

"I'm safe. I'm okay."

James was having trouble focusing, and he was still growling.

Kaylee slid her hands up his chest until she could cup his face. When he didn't look at her, she gave into frustration and caught hold of him by the ears, tugging sharply to get his attention.

His bear stared back.

"I'm going for a run," she said as haughtily as possible. "Maybe if you catch me we can have a discussion about your behaviour tonight."

His arm swung out as if he would grab her in an enormous hug, but she wasn't a cat for nothing. She dropped to the floor, and with a quick finger wave at her friends, headed for the exit.

Somebody in the crowd was alert enough to realize she needed a little help, shoving the door open then darting out of the way. It was a good thing, because she was using both hands to tear off her shirt. She made it through the opening and hung a hard right, all but throwing herself to the ground as she jerked off her skirt, kicked off her boots and shifted.

James was seconds behind her. Somebody must've

gotten in his way for long enough to give her that much of a head start, but it was enough. She raced toward the path conveniently located at the side of the parking lot. The one that headed into the wilderness, with multiple hunting trails and jogging paths for when the human community wanted to get out into the great outdoors as well.

Warm air rushed past her. Kaylee took deep breaths and let the distance vanish beneath her feet. She would've been quicker on snow, but the thick padding on her paws let her cover the branch-strewn spaces between the trees as she darted from one path to the next, leading James away from anyone he might get in trouble for decapitating.

She slowed and ducked around a tree—and damn near bumped into him, his massive bulk sitting in the middle of the path like a door stop.

Kaylee backpedaled, darting away and through a patch of prickly brambles, ducking low enough that she could fit without losing more than a few tufts of fur.

She ran through the open space on the opposite side as rapidly as possible, looking to get ahead of him. He'd have to go around the entire area, and the extra distance would give her time to—

Only, when she popped back out on the trail, he was there, lying across the path as if he were a Playboy model. One furry leg bent up and crossed over another, head supported on a paw.

He's cute, her cat said. *He's not supposed to be that cute. Cute, but oh so annoying.*

I'd kiss him, her cat said with shocking agreeability.

Which changed things to the nth degree. Her cat rarely liked anyone *that* way. Kaylee padded over to where James was waiting, now rolled onto his belly, watching her closely.

What the hell? Kaylee let her wild side do what she wanted, which was to nip the tip of his ear.

James batted his enormous powerful paw against her so delicately he wouldn't have disturbed the wings on a butterfly.

Quickly, she was shifting, and so was he, as he pulled her into his arms and brought her to the ground with him. He kept his body under hers, taking her lips possessively. The low rumble that had been pouring from his chest finally faded away after he'd kissed her hard enough to leave her gasping.

She knelt over him, palms pressed to his naked torso, staring down into his big brown eyes. "I don't need you to hurt people for me," she scolded.

"But he touched you," James repeated the phrase like a toddler with a one-track mind.

She tweaked his nose. "He did not. I protected myself."

"He could have hurt you."

Very doubtful. "Lara was like some high-test bodyguard on speed, so even if he had made contact, she would've had him on the ground in only seconds."

His expression turned to sheer confusion. "Lara did that?"

"Yes. And your brothers took care of another two, although that was because you were already a little busy taking out a dozen people on the direct route." When he blinked and had the grace to look a little ashamed, she leaned closer, thrilling as the heat of their chests. "I'm okay, I swear it."

He dipped his chin unsteadily, gaze rising to meet hers. "I think it's the mating bond. I mean, I've never felt like that before, so out of control."

She did another internal systems check, but there was

nothing different other than the fading traces of fear, annoyance, and amusement. The absolute terror on Alex's face as he spotted sweet Lara all but ready to skin her victim alive had been a great visual.

No mystical mating bond had snapped into place between her and James.

Still, she didn't want him worried about it. "I'm sorry you got caught by surprise like that. And while I don't feel anything, I understand. We'll be extra careful until things settle down."

James rolled, pinning her under him. The soft green moss under her back had been warmed by the sun, and with him lying over her, all sorts of interesting ideas were beginning to arise.

She reached down and wrapped her hands around his cock, stroking gently.

His eyes rolled back in his head and he groaned. "Kaylee."

"What? We had a nice run, and you caught me. I think that means you get a reward." She was longing to take him in her mouth. Longing to get to taste every bit of him once again.

What she got was a man on the edge, his hands moving in inspired ways as he teased and drove her wild. Playing with her breasts, tickling along her ribs, stroking between her legs.

She did her best to tease back, pushing him so she could rise up and nip at his shoulder. She dragged her teeth along the thick muscle of his neck then pressed a kiss to his chest, his torso scalding hot.

Her hands steady around his cock, stroking. His fingers deep inside her, sliding in and out in a way that teased of what would come.

She would. He would. They definitely would.

"Kaylee," James rumbled a warning as she slipped out from under him and turned her back. Dropping to her hands and knees, she cast a come-hither glance over her shoulder.

He laid a hand on her hip as he moved in behind her. Hands sliding up her back then down again. A caress that was worshipful and yet a demand. "I could stare at you for hours."

She did one better. "Don't stare. Fuck me."

His entire body shook at the dirty demand. He rocked against her, the thick length of his cock between her legs, her body wet and growing wetter as the solid head of his shaft bumped her clit over and over. "Tell me you want me."

"Yes. Now." She tilted her hips. His forward motion angled him between her folds, and this time he slid deep. All the way in until his hips met her backside.

Oh my God, so good. So full, so connected.

James panted hard. His fingers dug into her hips as he pulled back and thrust forward. Pace quickening, pressure deepening. Kaylee dropped onto her elbows and braced herself as he pounded into her. Every bit of her body tingled with awareness, rushing toward completion. When he bent over her, his body warm and protective, and one hand slid over her belly to land on her clit, she started a countdown.

Three, two—

"*James.*" Her sex clamped down on his cock, squeezing out pulses hard enough her limbs were ready to melt into the ground like spring runoff.

He jerked behind her, roaring his pleasure so loudly anyone within a five-mile radius probably heard him.

She couldn't find it in her to be embarrassed. Not one bit.

Still connected, James curled up, somehow finishing in a seated position with her impaled on his thick length. Their arms tangled around each other. Slightly sweaty, very sated.

She dropped her head on his chest and listened to his heart pound. "Great date," she finally got out.

His laughter rumbled up from his chest until the two of them were shaking.

He tucked his fingers under her chin and lifted until he was smiling down at her. "The best."

17

The next week passed in a blur. James was kept hopping getting ready for the gala.

Added to that, booking upcoming summer promotional tours had become increasingly difficult. Invitations were coming in that had to be answered. What he wanted to do was accept for himself and Kaylee.

Instead he sent them off as him with a plus one and hoped like hell they would find a way to make this work.

Truth was, he wanted her by his side. Always.

Not only in the apartment, where they'd fallen into a routine of waking in each other's arms, fooling around, then making breakfast together, both of them grinning from ear to ear.

Not only when she joined him as they went for walks in their human forms and runs in their animal forms.

Not only when they spent time with Alex and Cooper, his brothers watching carefully as if wanting to protect their baby sibling from being hurt.

Kaylee cared about him. He *knew* that. He knew that to the core of his being.

But they weren't mates. That box of potential inside him remained firmly wrapped, no matter how clearly he could sense it was real.

Which meant she was worried about everything she'd need to do as his mate, and it didn't seem he could do anything to reassure her on that count.

"I don't want to mess up anything for Borealis Gems," she repeated for the umpteenth time. "If I go up on a stage with you, who knows what might happen? I might have a panic attack. I might faint dead away—wouldn't that look good on national television?"

He squeezed her tightly. "What if you *don't* panic because I'm there beside you? Or what if you don't go up on the stage with me in the first place? You could be somewhere near the side and wave."

"Yeah, right. Perfect idea. I can see Meghan doing that with Prince Harry. Standing somewhere away from the crowd and waving when they call her name. Or sitting in the car and sticking an arm out instead of being by his side."

James had to grin.

She glared. "What's that expression for? We're talking about something serious here."

He couldn't help himself. "I like being compared to Prince Harry. And I think you and Meghan have a lot in common."

Her lips twitched. "You're such a pain," she complained softly, sliding into his arms and patting his chest.

"But I'm your pain, yes?"

Her lips twisted into a smile. "Yes."

Still, they hadn't come to any great solutions because while he honestly didn't mind keeping her out of the spotlight, it was clear that she needed to be there.

If he was choosing her to be his mate—*and he was*—he was choosing for her to be by his side.

Which meant...

A thought flickered across his brain too quickly for it to register.

Maybe he was thinking about this the wrong way. He struggled to figure out what was teasing in the back of his mind, but the next thing he knew it was the day of the gala, and his brave, sweet, beautiful Kaylee was sitting opposite him at the breakfast table as if she were preparing to face a firing squad.

He opened his mouth.

She held up a hand. "Not one word. I said I would be there for you, and I meant it."

"I want to protect you," he said sincerely. "That means I don't want you doing anything that's going to hurt."

"I get that, and I appreciate it so, so much. But you said something the other day that was true. What if?" She lifted tired eyes to his, but there was determination there as well. "What if the things I'm worried about are only in my head? What if I can do this, but I give up before I even try? That's not fair to you. So—let's do this."

He caught her fingers in his, squeezing tight before lifting them to his lips and kissing them tenderly. "That's my Kaylee Kat."

She slid out of her chair and crawled into his lap, and if he hadn't set a timer on his watch to remind him when he needed to be heading out, her sweet kisses would've made him late.

Kaylee walked with him to the door of the apartment, hand in hand.

"I'll be somewhere near the outdoor stage for most of

the day. We won't move into the auditorium until after eight," James reminded her.

"I'll find you. I'll get changed then join you."

James kissed her, tenderness in his heart as she squeezed his neck tightly before letting go, pacing back into the apartment as if she belonged there.

Which she did. She totally did, mating bond be damned.

Down at the fairgrounds, the car lot was beginning to fill as people wandered in the park, picking up food at the various vendors. There were families everywhere, with pockets of teenagers stealing into less supervised corners to flirt. It seemed the entire community had come out to the event.

He was in the middle of organizing a set of prizes when her call came through. "Kaylee. Where are you?"

"Late. I'm sorry, I'm not going to be there right at the opening."

The noises of the fair were slowly rising, and he slid away from the group he'd been working with to try and find quiet. "You need some help?"

She hesitated for a moment, then spoke crisply. "Small commitment popped up. It'll take me a couple of hours to take care of, and then I'll be there. I promise."

He found a quiet spot and focused on her. Listening intently to see if there was anything more she wanted to say.

Nothing.

He took a deep breath and trusted.

"I'll miss you," he shared. "I'm looking forward to seeing you, but I'm looking forward more to after the celebration is done. I plan to take you home and hold you all night long."

"I'd like that," she told him. "Now, go. I'm sure you've

got a million people needing you to help them. I'll get there as quick as I can."

Screw what everybody else thought. He blew her a kiss, smiling as her laugh carried over the line before she hung up.

Even with more than enough to do, Kaylee stayed on his mind. James worked quickly, smiling at people, chatting and being friendly. Eyeing the growing crowds.

Amber's familiar dark hair appeared as she exited the organizers' tent. James was surprised to see Lara at her side, her long silvery white hair pulled back into a high ponytail.

The women wandered slowly. James watched with interest to see more than one person give a double-take at spotting a member of Midnight Inc. at the Borealis Gems sponsored-event.

Including, it seemed, his brother.

"What's that woman doing here?" Alex demanded.

James shrugged. "It appears Amber and Kaylee have adopted her. You should probably get your nose back in joint, or the three of them are going to make your life hell for the sheer fun of watching you get annoyed."

"I don't trust her."

"I don't see that she's doing anything untrustworthy," James pointed out. He pivoted his head toward the parking lot, checking the open space beside his car in the hopes Kaylee's truck had magically appeared in the last three seconds.

"It's just not right," Alex complained as he folded his arms over his chest. "Inviting someone from the competition to hang around when I'm damn sure they're up to no good—"

"Maybe you need to keep a close eye on her," James suggested. Anything to get his brother out of his hair.

"I plan on it." Alex turned his scowl in James's direction. "Where's Kaylee?"

Great. The distraction failed. "She'll be here," James said mildly.

Alex checked his watch. "The first event starts in under ten minutes," he pointed out.

"Thank you, Big Ben."

"Just saying. Kaylee is usually more punctual than this..." Alex trailed off as he frowned. "Hang on. Kaylee is punctual, but she doesn't usually come to events like this. Are you sure?"

The look of concern on his brother's face was annoying to the extreme. "I said she'll be here."

But as the afternoon faded into evening and there was no sign of Kaylee, James found it harder to maintain a happy expression every time Alex gave him a pointed look.

He went up on the stage as he normally would, by himself, proclaiming the start of children's races and handing out prizes. All the things he'd done a million times. When he needed help, Amber stepped forward as always to offer a spare pair of hands, but it wasn't what he wanted.

Something must've happened. He checked his phone for the millionth time. There were no messages, but he kept hoping. Kept trusting.

She would be there. She'd promised, and Kaylee had never broken a promise to him. Not once in all the years that they'd been friends.

Come on, Kaylee, I need you by my side.

18

Earlier that morning...

aylee finished getting dressed in the quiet of James's apartment. The dread in her stomach disappeared quicker than she thought possible. Maybe all those *what ifs* that had jammed into her brain were actually working their way through far enough to make a difference.

She was scared silly to head to the gala and be expected to act as a master of ceremony, but for James, she was willing to try.

One quick stop and she'd join him. And hey, if nothing else, she could stress-eat cotton candy all afternoon until she had a reason for throwing up later.

She slipped into the post office and waved at the front desk staff, darting around the corner to peek into her box.

One parcel pickup and a delivery notice requesting her signature. Strange, or at least it was until she remembered that her parents were planning on inflicting something on her.

Nope. She wasn't having any of it. She would ignore the delivery notice for now. Maybe if it worked in their plans later this week, she and James would head out to her parents' house in the country and see if there was anything left to be moved.

Rebellion in hand, she was feeling pretty perky as she headed to the front desk, the parcel pickup notification flapping in her fingers. She even whistled a little bit.

Kaylee handed over the card. "You have something for me?"

"One here, and more." The postmaster reached behind her to grab a box off the shelf. "This small one fit in the office, but the rest of them—took two trucks to get everything out to the main address. Bit of a surprise. Sign here, please."

"My parental units are nothing if not unexpected," Kaylee said. Drat. She hadn't managed to completely avoid entanglement, but nothing said she had to go out to check the delivery today. She signed the paper a bit more cheerfully before accepting the box that was not much larger than a bread basket.

"Have a great day," the postmaster called as Kaylee stepped outside, swinging the light package in her hand—

The package shrieked.

It took everything in her to stop from dropping the box instantly. Kaylee ignored the few tourists wandering the street as she lowered the box to the ground and examined it more closely. There were small holes under the top edge of the lid, disguised by a layer of protective material that was wrapped over the entire thing. Kaylee had to look hard but finally found latches that allowed her to open a small corner of the box.

Shock raced through her.

Shiny black eyes and a black nose poked up into the small opening. A little mouth with jagged teeth opened in a teeny *meow*.

"Oh my God, they mailed me a kitten."

Kaylee examined the box for any kind of a message while the teeny thing behind the cage bars cried piteously. Beyond food and water dispensers, though, there was nothing else in the crate.

"It's okay, baby. I'll get you out of there in a minute. I need to find out what my idiot parents were thinking."

It took a couple minutes for Kaylee to settle the creature down before she could pull it out and nestle it in her lap. Black and tan markings made it look like some kind of Bengal tiger—not a shifter, obviously, considering the size of it.

When the tiny beastie finally curled up in a small fluffy puddle in her lap, Kaylee pulled out her phone and frantically opened her email.

Sure enough, one had arrived from her parents barely fifteen minutes ago.

Friend of a friend in the US informed us of a really good deal on these caps, so we decided to purchase them all and have them shipped north from New York State. Your father plans to purchase a logo machine so we can start up a sports enthusiast paraphernalia shop.

Toss everything in the shop until we get back, there's a good girl. I don't expect it will be any later than the fall, or possibly the new year.

Keep us up-to-date if you manage to find a job. Or if you

*plan to go back to school. We're always eager to encourage
your scholastic achievements.*

*Smooches.
Mother and father.*

She read the note three more times, but it never made
any more sense. *What on earth?* It certainly wasn't a *cap*
curled up in her lap.

What if all the boxes out at the house were the same?
What if by some freak mistake, her parents had sent a
delivery of live animals into the wilderness?

She stared at the message, cursed loudly, then opened
her phone. There was no way she could go with her original
plan and simply ignore the boxes. Not if living things might
suffer as a consequence.

Only, considering everything that James had to
coordinate today and the magnitude of the gala, she didn't
want him dropping everything to come and help her.

Heck, she didn't even know if she needed help. No, she
kept her cool and calmly told him she was going to be a late
without once letting him know she was in the middle of a
potentially weird situation.

Her heart turned over a little at the end of what she
thought was an amazingly reasonable conversation when he
blew her a kiss. Stupid how hard her heart thumped as she
pictured him doing it. Her big oversized bear being all cute
and puckering up for her.

Then she got in her truck and headed out to her
parents' house, a baby tiger nestled in her lap.

It was sound asleep at the end of the nearly hour-long
drive, so she took off her sweater and left the creature curled

up in a nest of soft fabric. She parked her truck in the shade and left the window cracked open so the little creature would be safe.

Then she went to work on the stack of boxes sitting out on the front porch where they were about to be hit by the sun.

Caps? No.

Cats? Definitely. Of all shapes and sizes.

They'd been shipped in large, roomy crates with food and water, but it was definitely time to give them room to roam. A few oversized kitty litter boxes would be handy, as well.

Kaylee debated for all of three seconds before making a decision that was going to really piss off her parents.

She unlocked the first crate and scooped out a pair of Siamese cats. "Welcome to Chez Feline. Make yourself at home."

She opened the door of the house and let them in.

It took hours because Kaylee had to make sure every one of them had access to water and found their own space to settle. Plus, she searched the entire house to find what was available that would make good kitty chow.

Thankfully, her parents had left a fully loaded supply of meat in the freezer. Everybody liked a good filet mignon.

It was good that Kaylee didn't have to leave the cats cooped up, because while she couldn't understand what they were saying, she read feline body language just fine. Getting free rein of the house turned their pissed-off attitudes into wild curiosity.

"I will get help as soon as the gala is done," she promised, leaving the door to the garage open. She'd created the world's biggest litter box by emptying emergency sandbags into a hastily created square.

Maybe it was her sincerity, or maybe the cats sensed she was reaching the end of the line, because miraculously, they settled peacefully, each one claiming different areas of the house for their own.

Every time she opened the door and came in, they watched. Dozens and dozens of eyes tracking her every move. If she hadn't been a cat herself, she would've been massively creeped out. As it was, she stopped and glared once or twice. Not to be mean, but to make sure they knew who was top dog in the room—so to speak.

The biggest crates contained wild animals nearly as big as James in his shifted form.

Kaylee folded her arms over her chest and held a staring contest with the biggest of them. The midnight black of the wild animal's fur was marked with the faint tracings of a panther.

When the panther blinked first, Kaylee let out a sharp snarl then opened her cage. The animal offered no resistance, striding by Kaylee's side into the house where she immediately made her way to the oversized couch, claiming it as her territory.

The rest of the full-sized wildcats cooperated in the same way.

Kaylee wiped the sweat from her brow as she refilled another set of bowls with water. It was a lot later than she'd hoped, but there was plenty of time for her to make it to the gala to be with James.

She turned and addressed the room. "Make yourselves at home, I'll be back later. No fighting," she warned, "or you'll all be grounded."

The panther on the couch yawned lazily, one paw draped over the armrest. Her tail swayed slightly as the baby Bengal played catch with it.

Kaylee slipped outside and locked the door behind her. She had a passing thought that this would not be a good day for a burglar to break in.

She was still giggling over that mental image when she went to turn the key in her truck. The engine squealed in protest right before it clicked three times and fell absolutely silent.

A set of swear words that would have made James proud flew from her lips. Kaylee didn't bother to try to open up the hood because she knew nothing about trucks other than the last time she'd heard that noise, it had cost her over a thousand dollars and taken three weeks to get the parts.

There was no choice. She slammed the door closed and stomped to the front porch. Stripping off her sweaty clothing was a bit of a relief, to be truthful. She smelt like wet cat, and that wasn't a pleasant aroma whether it was her or someone else's problem.

She put her feet on the grass and took a deep breath. Eyeing the sky for a moment, she knew daylight wasn't going to be a problem. It was distance. There wasn't a great shortcut between her parents' house and the fairgrounds. The straightest line put a whole bunch of water in the way.

Support came from the most unexpected of quarters. Her inner cat sighed mightily, but urged her on.

You told the bear you'd be there. Get your tail in gear, the beast ordered.

There's a lot of water in our way, Kaylee pointed out.

We can *swim. We just don't* like *to swim.* Her cat nodded decisively. *Just don't make this a habit. Not even for the cute furry one.*

Kaylee snickered but agreed, wondering what James would think of his new nickname. She repeated it back as a promise. *Not even for the cute furry one.*

She shifted, then ran toward the man she loved.

Toward the man who was probably wondering why she wasn't already by his side.

19

_A_s the afternoon slipped into evening, James's faith that Kaylee would be there never faltered. It didn't matter how many looks Alex gave him, and it didn't matter that he caught Amber staring at him with a sad expression.

"She'll be here," he told the human woman bluntly.

Amber smiled sweetly. "I'm sure there's a good reason why she hasn't arrived yet."

"I hope she's not in trouble," James muttered, checking his phone for the millionth time as he once again attempted to message her.

He was all but stalking her online, and he hated that, but at the same time, he was worried. This wasn't about needing her help at the gala or trying to figure out how they were going to go forward while not being mates—although the mate thing was a nonissue.

He felt it. That box inside.

What's more, he could've sworn that an hour ago something had adjusted. As if the ribbon tied around the box had loosened off, and he was one step closer to seeing what was inside.

Still, his watch said it was now nearly nine o'clock. They'd moved the gala inside and switched from casual family picnicking to grown-up dancing with endless champagne and expensive hors d'oeuvres.

He wore a suit that he knew fit well, and he was dashing and ready to charm. But as he walked through the crowds and accepted handshakes and pleased smiles, there were also curious glances and questions about where Kaylee was.

It was killing him.

He briefly joined Alex and Cooper at the base of the stairs that led to the stage, taking a deep breath and closing his eyes as he let it out slowly.

A heavy hand landed on his shoulder. Cooper. Solid and reassuring. "I'm sure she'll be here soon."

A low grumble escaped Alex followed by a gasp.

James opened his eyes to discover Alex rubbing his shoulder. Cooper shook out his fingers as if his fist had recently been in action. His older brother glared meaningfully.

"Fine. I'm sure Kaylee is safe as well, but I'm mad at her, okay?" Alex admitted. "I hate to see you like this, bro."

"See me how?" James asked.

Alex shrugged. "I know you said you chose her, but today's the loneliest I've seen you in a long time. It's not right. I like Kaylee plenty, but if she's not able to be there for you, something's got to change."

Like a switch being thrown and the light coming on, that was all it took. The missing bit of information. The idea that had eluded him.

James's heart beat wildly, smashing against his rib cage. He slammed his hands down on Alex's shoulders and squeezed tight, sheer joy rushing his veins. "You're absolutely right."

Alex cringed as James's hands made impact—probably figured he was about to be taken apart by one pissed-off bear. Instead, James hauled him in for a tight hug, pounding him between the shoulders before shoving him away and grabbing hold of Cooper. He offered his oldest brother the same enthusiastic back-pounding before stepping away. "You guys are the best. I mean that."

Cooper's expression turned suspicious. "What are you up to?"

"Making a change," James announced before whirling. He took the stairs three at a time, only slowing when he reached the edge of the auditorium stage.

Grandpa Giles was holding court in the middle of the stage. The spotlight on the debonair gentleman turned him into the feature presentation at a rock star's sold-out farewell tour.

But alert as usual, he spotted James and motioned him forward. "There he is. I guess it's time for me to stop boring you all with my stories. I'll let my grandson carry on the festivities. James?"

Grandpa Giles held his arms out welcomingly. James marched forward. He took the old man's hand and shook it while out in the audience, polite applause rose.

James took control of the microphone, but then when his grandpa would've walked away, James held him back.

"Before I get started, I wanted to say a few words to my grandpa." James knew how to work a crowd, and if there was ever a time to do it, this was it.

Maybe Kaylee wasn't there, yet she *was*. She was there in his heart, and while he needed to get this done so he could get off the stage and go find her, there was something important that had to be accomplished first.

He looked his grandpa in the eyes and offered a wink,

just to get the old man wondering, before he turned to the audience before him. "Not all of you have the pleasure of a close-knit family like mine. I'll tell you that usually it's a wonderful thing. Although occasionally..." He pulled a face, tilting his head as he looked out over the invisible crowd before him.

A trickle of laughter rose.

"But between the rare times we don't get along, and the many times that we do, there's something that binds us all together. Borealis Gems, it's a true family operation. You all know my oldest brother, Cooper, and my brother Alex are involved with the intricate details of running the place on a daily basis. My parents, although not here in Canada, are doing what they can to help out, looking for new sources and making sure that everything is being done in a way that's ecologically sound and follows the family mandate. Because that's important to us here at Borealis Gems."

Applause again, this time stronger with a few shouts of approval.

James glanced back at his grandpa, his grandma waiting in the wings with curiosity on her face. "Here is part of the reason why we have such a strong family ethic. This man, my grandpa. He's the one who taught all of us the business. He taught me how to tell a joke, how to pick the perfect setting for the perfect situation. Hell, he taught me how to fish. With a rod, and with the paw—and if you want a good story, ask him to tell you about the time we got caught in a flash flood up on the White River in the Yukon."

Grandpa Giles wore a huge grin. He shook his head, waggling a finger in James's direction.

The sweet sensation inside James's chest was growing. As if something was unraveling. The need to go find Kaylee increased until it was a pulse inside his body, urgent. Dire.

It was a good thing he was nearly done, yet he owed it to his brothers and the family to finish this properly. "Yes, everybody needs to have somebody in their life like Grandpa Giles. Not only does he teach us things, but he's one of those people who light a fire under you and make you do the right thing even when you don't feel like it at the time. Which is why right now, before all of you, I want to say thank you, Grandpa Giles. Thanks for your leadership and guidance and encouragement, I couldn't have done it without you."

He glanced over at the wings of the stage where Cooper and Alex had moved into the very edge of the light. He met their eyes steadily. Alex looked worried. Cooper seemed rock solid as if he suspected what James was about to do. He dipped his chin in approval.

James took a deep breath and turned back to his grandpa. "I'm handing in my resignation, effective immediately."

A gasp went up from the crowd. Grandpa Giles blinked, his mouth opening and closing, but no words came out.

Wow. Amazing. It was a moment to savour. It wasn't often that anyone managed to make the old man speechless.

But James didn't have time. Somewhere out there Kaylee needed him, and this was only one step in doing the right thing.

It was time to finish it. James spoke to the crowd in the auditorium again. "I'll continue working for the company, but in some other role. You see, while up until now I've been a son, a grandson, and a brother, I recently added a new title to the list. I want to be able to spend time with my mate, and that requires a change. She's the most important thing in my world—family is still high on my list, but my

Kaylee is at the very top. I can't wait to see what each day I get to spend with her brings."

There was a crash to the side of the stage.

James glanced over to discover Kaylee standing beside his brothers.

There were leaves in her hair, the long strands plastered across her face in wet strands. She was naked except for a brightly coloured swatch of fabric wrapped around her body like a toga.

Mud streaked her face, lines of it covering her knees and arms. There was a dark blob clinging to the tip of her nose, but most importantly, she was *there*, staring at him with wonder in her eyes.

She was the most beautiful woman he'd ever seen.

20

Kaylee didn't know her feet were moving at first. Nothing registered except that tug deep inside that said she needed to be next to James. Right. Damn. Now.

Next to the big bear shifter who owned her heart, body, and soul.

It had taken forever to run the distance between her parents' and the fairgrounds. Three of the rivers she had to cross had been swollen to excess with spring runoff, leaving her an exhausted mess by the time she made it across the distance.

Then once she'd shifted, the only thing she could find to pull on had been the banner hanging across the front gate. Beggars couldn't be choosers, and she'd ripped it from its moorings, wrapped it around her body and raced for the auditorium in time to hear James give up everything for her.

This wasn't how she'd planned to notch up her shaky confidence. She was supposed to be perfectly groomed and dressed like a princess, but it didn't matter.

None of that mattered, because James stood in front of her with love in his eyes, his arms outstretched.

Screw it. She didn't need to impress anyone but him and clearly, he was going to be a sacrificial bastard if she didn't get a move on.

She paced across the stage, her feet leaving wet prints behind.

His gaze never wavered, but his smile grew broader, and his hand rose to cover his chest, fingers spread wide as if attempting to contain his heart.

There were a million things she could say. There were a million things she should be worried about, but none of them mattered even a fraction as much as the one thing pounding through her brain.

She stopped directly in front of him, staring into his eyes. "I love you, James Borealis."

He slipped off his suit jacket, sliding it around her shoulders, staying in contact, his touch warm through the layers of fabric. "Convenient, because I love you too."

Shock waves of joy raced, but it wasn't enough. Kaylee took a deep breath then stole the microphone from his hand. "Grandpa Giles?"

The old man stood only a few feet to the side, amusement written on every inch of his face. "Yes, darling?"

"I need you to pretend you didn't hear a word James said during the last five minutes. I mean, remember the part where he loves me, but not the quitting nonsense." She took a deep breath, braced herself, then turned to look at the crowd.

Shockingly, she saw nothing but darkness, the house lights shining in her eyes. It left her blind in a way, but somehow, she knew that if she could see each individual face in the crowded room, she now had the courage to deal with it.

"Hello, everyone. I assume you're out there. If I could have your attention, please. I also need you to pretend you didn't hear that last bit. Of course, James is not stepping down from his role at Borealis Gems. He's the most wonderful spokesman they could have, and incredibly knowledgeable about the history of the company and the direction it's going in the future. If any of you have questions or want to arrange publicity events, you'll want to make an appointment soon before he gets booked up."

There was a rumble of laughter, disconnected voices, and soft amusement, and yet instead of freaking her out, it felt a little like sharing stories with James in the dark.

Those days so long ago when they used to camp in the backyard, and she'd lie in the tent and he'd lie outside so he could shift to his bear form without messing with zippers.

She hadn't been able to see him then either, but as they'd stay up late to tell stories and share secrets, she'd always known he was there. Guarding her. Caring for her.

Learning how to love her.

Every bit of their past made it easy to keep going. "You'll definitely want to make your bookings as soon as possible because part of what he said was right. I hope to be occupying more of his time. You see, James was trying to be gallant for my sake. That's why he was going to give up the job that he is so perfect for, but it's my turn to do the right thing. Somehow, I'm going to figure out what needs to be done so I can be by his side and help *him*. I know I can do it, because James has told me I can."

She faced him. James, who she could see perfectly. James, who was the center of her universe, now and always, the way it was supposed to be.

"He hasn't only told me recently, though. He started years ago. Everything he's done, and all the time we've spent together, affirmed how much he cares about me and how proud he is of all the things I've accomplished. How certain he is that I'm capable of doing anything I put my mind to."

James stepped toward her.

Kaylee took a deep breath. "Sometimes it's scary to step out from behind the camera or step into a new relationship. But when your best friend tells you you've got the balls to do it, you have to believe the guy."

The ripple of laughter that burst free from the darkness sparkled like fireworks, but Kaylee barely registered it because James had caught her fingers in his hands. He tugged her body against his as he slid an arm around her torso and held on tight.

"Does this mean you'll stop arguing with me?" he teased, his voice going softer.

She clicked off the power on the microphone. "In your dreams, Borealis."

James tilted his head. "Then what are you saying, Banks?"

"I think..." She slid a hand up his chest until her palm rested over where his heart beat as rapidly as her own. "I think I'm perfect for you, even if I'm not your mate. I'm yours, you're mine. I *choose* to believe that one hundred percent with everything in me. I'm going to do everything I can to love you with every bit of me. Always—"

A sudden storm hit the stage. James grabbed hold of her and tucked her head against his body as a whirlwind swept out of nowhere. Her hair fluttered around them, lights flashed, and there was a rumble under her feet that set their bodies trembling.

Inside her, something tumbled. A set of dominoes,

spiraling outward until the tingling sensation that started in her core reached her fingers and toes, reaching for James as if to tangle him in a spider web right next to her. The two of them, together. Wrapped up tight, side by side...

No—

It was far more than that. They were connected. Together.

One.

Oh wow.

James's grin grew wider if that was even possible. "Holy *shit*."

It was clear they were not alone, because spontaneous applause burst out from behind them, echoing off the walls of the auditorium and filling the space with the rumble of approval.

None of that mattered because the only thing Kaylee felt was him. Connected to her inside and out and surrounded and together in the midst of the storm.

She clutched the front of his shirt. "James? Does this mean—?"

"That we're mates?" His voice sounded in her head and she wanted to cry from sheer joy. *"Seems that way."*

Giddiness rocked her as she tried to respond back using the incredible, unbelievable brand-new connection between them. *"Go ahead, tell me I told you so."*

He slid his hand around the back of her neck, tangling his fingers in her messy hair. He brushed their noses together. Lips barely touching. Wind still whirling at their backs.

"I told you that I chose to keep you forever. I think you owe me something big for this."

How was it possible for her to be able to sense his teasing tone, even in her brain?

She curled her arms around him and pressed their bodies together tight. "I'm pretty sure I can think of something," she promised.

He pulled back, and she laughed out loud, her hand flying up to cover her mouth.

James frowned. "What?"

She reached out to brush mud off his nose. "You're a mess, and I love you."

He caught hold of her fingers and turned her toward the side of the stage. The unnatural whirlwind calmed, leaving papers from the podium scattered across the stage floor.

Grandpa Giles made his way over, gathering the mess as he walked. His suit jacket and tie were rumpled, and he smoothed them back into place as he nodded with approval at James and Kaylee.

Then he motioned them off as if he were chasing an unruly cat from the room—

Oh. Cats.

She tugged on James's arm as they made their way off the stage, thundering applause echoing after them. "We're going to need a little help," she warned him. "You're not going to believe the reason I was late."

He pressed his lips to the back of her hand, guiding her toward where his brothers stood. "I know it was a good reason, but even more, I knew you'd come to me."

Cooper scooped her up and spun her in a circle, squeezing her tight before pressing a brotherly kiss to her forehead as he placed her back on her feet. "Welcome to the family, although you've always been like a little sister to me."

"Slightly annoying, annoying, more than slightly annoying—" Alex said blandly. He made a face. "First, I apologize. James, I was wrong, and I'm glad."

Kaylee waited as the two brothers shook hands as if something somber had gone down.

Alex turned to her, his serious expression lightening. "Little sister. I'm glad you're with this jerk, but the next time you need help, *ask*. If you've got a problem, *we've* got a problem, understand? That's what family does."

Kaylee's throat tightened up again. "Thank you. Although you might regret that tomorrow," she warned, thinking about how all those cats were going to react when three polar bears showed up.

Alex gave her a quick hug, and then James was stealing her away, guiding her down secret back passages and around corners.

The sound of voices and party noise and music faded into the background. Kaylee held on tight to his warm hand and followed where he wanted to lead.

Tomorrow they would have to find places for dozens of wildcats. Tomorrow she'd have to look into getting her beater of a truck repaired, again. And maybe not tomorrow, but sometime in the near future she was going to have a long talk with her parents about what was and wasn't appropriate for them to ask her to do without a buy-in.

But that was all in the future.

This moment she was going with her mate somewhere secret. Somewhere alone.

Her mate, oh my God, her *mate*.

They'd just stepped into the open when Kaylee tugged him to a stop. A moment later she'd wrapped herself around him as laughter bubbled up inside. She held on to James as if she were never letting go.

He cupped her face with his hand. "I'm so glad fate finally came to her senses."

"You really think fate had a chance after James Borealis made a choice?" Kaylee shook her head.

He chuckled. "Maybe fate was out of luck from the moment Giles Borealis laid down the law in the first place."

"Your grandfather is a wonderful, bossy, *interfering* man." She grinned at the fire in James's eyes. "Although I'm not going to tell him the wonderful part. He doesn't need to have any more reasons to gloat."

James nodded decisively. "No matter what, we were meant for each other. There's no arguing that fact." As they stood there with the midnight sun shining down on them, a soft breeze brushing through his hair, he leaned in close. "I look forward to spending the rest of my life proving that to you, fate, and the entire world."

Then he kissed her.

EPILOGUE

*A*lex Borealis was tired, grumpy and frustrated. The perfect storm of emotions that would lead a lesser man into making a terrible mistake.

Oh, he knew exactly how he wanted to get rid of the adrenaline in his system, but since he prided himself on having discipline, what he wanted was not going to happen.

No way, no how would he let a pair of sparkling brown eyes with goldish flecks lead him astray. Instead, he used the hard labour of cleaning up the mess from the party to distract himself.

It was well after two a.m. before the final partygoers left the building. Vehicles remained in the parking lot to be picked up the next day. Guests who'd had a little too much to drink had decided against driving home. Instead, they'd shifted, a mass of tipsy bears, cats, and wolves teetering across the asphalt before disappearing into the trees.

Alex watched them go with something close to disapproval. He had no objections to having a little fun, but there was a time and a place for excess, and this wasn't it.

He came around the corner and jerked to a stop as he

met up with a skeleton cleanup crew putting away the last of the tables from the auditorium. "Amber. That thing is three times too big for you to carry," he scolded as he hurried across the floor. He caught the edge and attempted to tug it away from her with no success.

All he got for his troubles was a glare of annoyance.

"I already told her to stop, but she takes direction just about as well as you do," Cooper said dryly. "As in *not*."

"What a thing to say about your personal assistant," Amber offered perkily. "I live to serve you."

Cooper turned his back quickly, and Alex bit back a snicker. He didn't think Amber had spotted that his big brother actually flushed at her words.

Cooper needed to get out more if the little human's completely innocent comment ruffled him that hard.

Forget Cooper. We *need too*, his bear complained. *Where's the wolf?*

Shut up, Alex snapped at his inner self.

The beast snarled but quieted down.

Fifteen minutes later, Alex got the final report from all but one of his security team. He escorted Cooper and Amber to the exit, locking the door after them.

He was headed back into the building when his radio went off.

"Alex," he snapped.

"Nearly done." The final report coming in. "I need to do a sweep of the auditorium stairwell."

"I'll take it," Alex offered. "I'm right there."

"Thanks, boss." The man sighed happily. "Great evening. So happy for your brother."

"Yeah. It's a good thing," Alex offered before turning off his radio and heading at a brisk pace to complete the final check.

He made it down three flights of stairs before realizing that the scent in the air was growing stronger. The scent that had been subtly driving him mad for days, ever since he'd gotten stuck in the booth next to Lara Lazuli.

Anger rose inside him, partly at her, but mostly at himself. The scent of her made him want to pick her up and slam her against the nearest surface. Not to hurt her, but to rip her clothes off and take her as if he were some kind of wild animal.

Ummm, his bear began.

Shut. Up, Alex snapped.

There on the ground floor by the exit doors, he caught up with her. "What the hell do you think you're doing?"

Lara whirled, eyes wide, the silver rope of her hair flying to land across her chest. "*You.*"

He bore down on her like an elephant on a rampage. "What are you doing lurking in the corners? Try to get intel on Borealis Gems?"

"No," she said quickly. "I was helping Amber earlier, and I took off my shoes. I had to come back to get them."

A pair of three-inch heels dangled from her fingers, all sinfully thin silver straps and sexy buckles, and the thought of her in them made his body tighten in ways he didn't want to admit.

"I was working with Amber, and you weren't there," he growled, closing in on her.

"Yeah, because you were totally in the ladies' room where somebody had the bright idea to draw hearts on the mirrors in lipstick. Oh, I know you must've been hiding in one of the stalls while I was climbing up on the counter to help scrub the mirrors clean."

He glanced down. There were faint smudges on the knees of her capris.

He grabbed her hand, a gasp escaping her as he lifted it toward his face. He flipped her palm up, hesitating as he spotted pale pink streaks under her nails.

He met her gaze. "Why would you help clean up a mess at a Borealis Gems event?"

"Because I was spending time with a friend, and she needed a hand. So I figured I wouldn't be a dick and leave her with work to do by herself when I could help." She tugged her arm as if trying to escape his grasp. "But I guess you don't get that concept. Helping a friend."

The chaos in his gut swirled harder. He'd been a jerk, and he knew it. But it was be a jerk or admit how much he wanted this woman who was the last person on earth he should be with.

"Let go," Lara said quietly, as if all of the fight had gone out of her. Her head hung low.

Shockingly, intense concern hit hard.

"What's wrong?" Alex demanded.

She shook her head.

Dammit all. He put two and two together and came up with something he didn't like. He bet anything she was pulling a fast one. First on Amber, now on him.

Maybe it was time to throw a little bait. He caressed his thumb over the back of her hand, the softness making his entire body tighten with need. He shoved down his desire and focused on doing what was needed. He had to make sure Borealis Gems was safe. "I have no problem helping a friend."

Lara stiffened. Her head slowly tilted until her gaze met his. "Really?"

He spoke softly, intimately. Enticing her to share. "Of course. Tell me—there's something going on, isn't there?"

For one moment her eyes softened. Instead of tugging

away, her fingers wrapped around his as if she wanted to stay close. As if the sensation screaming through his veins that wanted him to strip her down and make her his was driving through her as well.

Heavy with desire, craving more.

She opened her mouth, and in the instant before she said something, the sensation he had won thrilled up his spine. She was going to spill the beans, and he hadn't truly committed to anything.

Lara went absolutely motionless. Her gaze flickered.

She licked her lips. Slowly.

He couldn't resist. He stared at her mouth hungrily, because having her this close, he could imagine what that tongue would feel like against his. What she would taste like.

What he could do to her to make them both howl.

Unexpectedly, she moved. She pressed herself against him and tangled her fingers in his hair. Something clattered to the floor—her shoes?—as she kissed him, hard, wild fire and need flaring in the instant before he reacted.

And react he did. The next thing he knew, they were fighting for control as he kissed her back as if possessed.

He didn't care. He picked her up, pressing her body against the nearest wall—and his inner bear rumbled with delight and a fair bit of gloating.

See? Animal. Go on...

Alex ignored the beast as best he could, sliding a foot to the side when his arm hit the intercom system for the building. Then it was all about her taste flooding his system, sexual tension rising at high velocity until he was nearly mad with want.

Lara scratched at his shoulders and tugged at his buttons until she succeeded in stripping away his shirt. He bent and licked the skin on her neck before biting lightly. She let out a soft scream and dug in her nails hard enough to leave marks, which only made the whole fucking thing that much hotter.

Alex swore, dragging his lips from her skin. "This is wrong. This is all wrong, but dammit, I want you."

She wiggled, and he set her down. Then her hands were on his waistline and she was working his button and zipper, pushing his pants from his hips, pressing him back toward the wall at the bottom of the stairwell.

He clutched the railing with both hands behind him to catch his balance. He had one foot on the first stair, the other on the landing as her hand dipped into his dress pants and her fingers wrapped around the hard length of his cock.

Alex's head fell back, smacking into the wall as she worked him through the fabric of his briefs.

This might be wrong, but no way could he tell her to stop. Pleasure rippled through his body even as he fought to regain control. She was pressed up against the side of him, one hand behind him, but it was the other hand that had one hundred percent of his attention because—

Holy freaking hotness.

The next thing he knew, Lara wrenched herself from him. She jerked to a stop four feet away and stared with an unreadable expression. Her chest rocked heavily as she panted, trying to catch her breath. She was all ruffled, strands of her hair having escaped her ponytail. Her clothes were messed up, shoes scattered on the floor by her feet.

Bare feet, with pale pink toenails.

"Come here," Alex ordered, reaching for her—

His hands jerked to a stop behind him.

He growled as he glanced down to discover he was cuffed in place. One loop was fastened around each wrist, and the chain between them tangled around the metal handrail at the side of the stairwell.

"What the hell is going on?" He lunged for her, but all he got for his troubles was a pain in his shoulders.

"They're your handcuffs. Figure it out." She scooped down and grabbed her shoes, patting her hair and straightening her clothing. "I'm glad you're willing to help your friends. But considering you didn't say *friends* included me, perhaps we should call this all a mistake. I hope you have a lovely evening."

She stepped to the exit doors before pausing to put her shoes back on. It wasn't right that his cock throbbed as he watched her slip into those fuck-me stilettos.

"You won't get away with this," he warned.

"I wasn't trying to get away with anything," she said softly. Almost sadly.

She tossed the key for the cuffs at his feet then slipped out the door.

What an impossible situation. With his hands behind his back Alex couldn't grab the keys to unlock himself. His pants slowly slid downward, pooling around his ankles.

One hell of a mess.

He watched her through the narrow sliver of glass in the exit door as she stepped over to a bright red Maserati parked beside his black Porsche. As she got into the vehicle, he swore that it was the last time Lara Lazuli was going to get the best of him. He had no idea how she'd managed to pick his pocket without him being aware of it—

But then again, he *had* been a little distracted.

That was another thing. Someday they were going to finish what they'd started, or his name wasn't Alex Borealis.

A loud buzz sounded, and he blinked in surprise until he realized a green light was flashing on the intercom system on the wall beside him. It was close enough that if he leaned over and used his nose, he could hit the talk button.

Awkward, but it worked.

"What?"

"Alex?" His gramps sounded far too perky for this time of night.

"*What?*" he repeated gruffly.

"Is that how you speak to your grandfather?" Grandpa Giles demanded. "I assume you're tired from the day, so I'm going to ignore your rudeness. I wanted to touch base, though, and figured you'd be the only one answering the intercom at this hour. Glad I caught you before you left the building."

Alex glanced down at the floor then at his hands trapped behind his back. "Yeah, I might be hanging out for a little longer."

"I won't keep you. You grandmother and I are heading to bed, but I wanted to let you know she's asked me to take this coming week off. And you know how much I love your grandma. I'll do anything for that woman."

"Including toss a job my direction that you should've been doing?" Alex drawled.

"Two o'clock meeting tomorrow," Grandpa Giles admitted. "You're always looking for information to upgrade security, and that's exactly what this meeting will provide. You keep on the cutting edge of what's available. I've always liked that about you, Alex. Hard to catch you with your pants down."

Alex took a deep breath and ignored the irony of the comment. "Of course, I can take the meeting for you. Two o'clock will be no problem." By that time, he'd have gnawed his wrist off if that was the only way to get out of the handcuffs. "Who's the meeting with?"

"You're going to have to be on your toes, boy. She's a tricky one. Never sure what's going on with the rest of that family, and her personality is probably boring as day old toast, but as far as security goes, she's brilliant."

This wasn't the night. "Gramps, stop talking in circles. What's her name, this paragon of virtue?"

"Lara Lazuli. Don't forget. Two o'clock. Don't be late."

Outside the exit window the taillights of the Maserati were slowly growing fainter as she drove away. Alex stared after her, a deep pulse racing through his system, and a whole lot of vengeance and sexual intention on his mind.

"I wouldn't miss it for the world."

~

New York Times Bestselling Author Vivian Arend
brings you a light-hearted paranormal trilogy
Borealis Bears

Get mated—or else!

When the meddling, match-making family patriarch lays
down the law, Giles Borealis' three polar bear shifter
grandsons agree to follow his edict. Only James, Alex and
Cooper each have a vastly different plan in mind to deal
with their impending mating fevers. Will any of them be
able to fight fate?

Spoiler: *not likely!*

~

Borealis Bears
The Bear's Chosen Mate
The Bear's Fated Mate
The Bear's Forever Mate

~

ABOUT THE AUTHOR

With over 2 million books sold, Vivian Arend is a *New York Times* and *USA Today* bestselling author of over 50 contemporary and paranormal romance books, including the Six Pack Ranch and Granite Lake Wolves.

Her books are all standalone reads with no cliffhangers. They're humorous yet emotional, with sexy-times and happily-ever-afters. Vivian pretty much thinks she's got the best job in the world, and she's looking forward to giving readers more HEAs. She lives in B.C. Canada with her husband of many years and a fluffy attack Shih-tzu named Luna who ignores everyone except when treats are deployed.

www.vivianarend.com